vesper

A DEVIANTS NOVEL

vesper

A DEVIANTS NOVEL

JEFF SAMPSON

Balzer + Bray
An Imprint of HarperCollins*Publishers*

Balzer + Bray is an imprint of HarperCollins Publishers.

Vesper: A Deviants Novel
Copyright © 2011 by Jeff Sampson
All rights reserved. Printed in the United States of America.
No part of this book may be used or reproduced in any manner whatsoever without written permission except in the case of brief quotations embodied in critical articles and reviews. For information address HarperCollins Children's Books, a division of HarperCollins Publishers, 10 East 53rd Street, New York, NY 10022.
www.harperteen.com

Library of Congress Cataloging-in-Publication Data is available.
ISBN 978-0-06-199276-6

Typography by Jennifer Rozbruch
11 12 13 14 15   LP/RRDB   10 9 8 7 6 5 4 3 2 1

First Edition

The Vesper Company
"Envisioning the brightest stars, to lead our way."
- Internal Document, Do Not Reproduce -

Partial Transcript of the Interrogation of
Branch B's Vesper 1
Part 1—Recorded Oct. 31, 2010

[A chair squeaks. A male coughs.]

F. Savage (FS): Testing. Say hello.

Vesper 1 (V1): Hi.

FS: Please state your name and age for the record.

V1: [clears throat] My name is Emily Webb. I am sixteen years old.

FS: And can you confirm that no one is forcing you to speak to me?

[Silence.]

FS: It can't record a shrug, Emily.

V1: Yeah, sorry. Sorry. Yes, I am recording this of my own free will.

FS: I have to say that I'm very glad you've overcome your initial resistance, Emily. You'll find that all we are asking is your help in forming a clearer picture of the events that took place prior to, ah, the incident.

V1: Before you kidnapped us, you mean?

FS: Erm, actually, I was referring to the unfortunate circumstances prior.

[Chains clang.]

V1: [sighs.] After I tell you everything, you'll let us go, right?

FS: Was that what you were told?

V1: It was kind of implied, yeah.

FS: I'll have to check on that for you, then. In the meantime, we should begin reviewing your written account. [Papers are shuffled.] You've managed to write a lot of pages since you've been here, Emily. [More paper shuffling.] A whole, uh—a whole lot of pages.

V1: Well, you asked me to write my story, so I thought—

FS: No, no, it's fine. It's just a lot to read. So let's review what we have. This is the account of the first week? Is that correct?

V1: Yeah. That's right.

FS: Where does it start? The events in here, that is.

V1: It starts the night Emily Cooke was killed. That was the first time I . . . the first time I became aware things weren't normal.

1

YOU'RE NOT GOING ALL JEKYLL AND HYDE, ARE YOU?

I was halfway out my bedroom window when my cell rang.

The ringtone was some ancient pop song from when I was twelve, the sound distorted and screechy. I was precariously balanced with one bare leg out the window and the other wedged against my desk chair. Now was definitely not the best time for a phone call.

I ignored it, and the song cut off abruptly as the call went to voice mail. In the phone's silent wake I could hear clearly the sounds of the night outside—the cool wind whistling past trees, a dog's barks echoing between houses, some road-raging driver laying on his horn down the street.

I needed to be out there. I wanted to dive into the darkness beyond my window, get filthy and carefree. Smiling, I started to push myself through my window.

The cell rang again.

Seriously, caller: horrendous timing.

I shoved a hand into my shorts and pulled out my cell. The screen was blurry, so I squinted. It read REEDY.

Reedy—my rail-thin best friend, Megan. My very persistent best friend, Megan.

I had *plans* and *so* didn't feel like talking . . . but this was Megan. I had to answer. Besides, I knew the whole persistent thing meant she wouldn't stop calling until I picked up.

I flipped open the cell and held it to my ear. "Hello?"

"Emily?" Megan's voice was jittery, anxious. "Is that you? Are you okay?"

"What?" Weird question. Of *course* I was okay. I was better than okay.

Something flitted past my window, some night bird swooping down to snatch up a rodent, maybe. My thoughts drifted away from Megan, from Megan's tone and her questions, back to the world outside.

It was as though the night had a smell. Some heavy scent that washed thickly over me and hovered in the air like beckoning fingers, as if I was in some old Looney Tunes cartoon. My body itched with the urge to leap out the window, hit the ground, and run.

"Emily?" Megan asked again. Her voice was too low, too intense, and the sound of it buzzed in my ear like a fly.

I shook my head and focused on the carpet inside my room. Splayed open on the floor was a book I'd dropped. Its words were fuzzy smudges on the pages. I vaguely recalled reading it earlier, but I had no memory of how it ended up thrown to the ground. That was . . . strange. Why had I dropped the book? What exactly was I in the midst of doing?

"You there?"

An itch to *do* something prickled over my limbs, and the wondering left me, washed away. I said, "It's me. What's up?"

From the other end came a sigh of relief. "You sounded like Dawn for a second. Want to hear what I heard?"

I didn't, really. I wanted to click off the phone and dive outside. Instead I said, "Sure."

"You hear anything about Emily Cooke?"

"What about her?"

"She got shot," Megan said flatly. "They just found her tonight, blocks and blocks away from her house. And get this, she was barefoot and in pajamas. No one has any idea what she was doing way out there. I heard it from that deputy in my brother's band—you know, the drummer guy."

My hand went limp, and I almost dropped the phone. My mind went woozy for just a moment, and the words on the book beneath me focused, became clear. Whatever had been beckoning me outside vanished, and the bare leg I had stretched over the window felt suddenly cold.

"They . . . found her?" I asked.

A pause on the other end, then, "You know, found. As in, her body."

"Oh."

I blinked. My eyes felt far too dry. Should I be crying? I didn't know Emily Cooke very well. We'd shared classes since elementary school and were the same age, but for the last nine years I'd only ever known her as "the other Emily." It had been annoying to always be confused with her by teachers each school year, but that annoyance felt stupid now.

"Are you still there?"

I nodded. Then, feeling like an idiot, I said, "I'm here. That's really awful. Poor Emily. Her poor parents . . ."

"Whatever, she was just some insipid rich girl who'd have grown up to be the next Paris Hilton, anyway." Megan's voice softened. "It was just . . . I heard 'Emily,' and 'dead,' and I freaked. It happened only a few streets away from where you live, and Em, I thought it was *you*. Lucas told me that it was Emily Cooke, but I had to call you and make sure."

"No, it wasn't me," I said. "I'm . . . fine."

Except, no. I wasn't fine at all.

"Well, okay. I'm glad you're okay, Em. See you in the morning. Seven thirty?"

"Yeah."

The phone clicked and I lowered it from my ear. My leg trembling, I started to pull myself back inside. Whatever it was that had made me want to jump out of my bedroom window was gone, and the dark outdoors seemed about as inviting as an off-season summer camp when a masked serial killer is on the prowl.

Feelings I didn't really understand washed over me, distracted me. Sort of like my brain was filled with air and making me woozy. I couldn't focus as I pulled myself inside and I lost my balance, toppling off the windowsill and onto the floor.

Graceful. And to think I used to want to be a ballerina.

Behind me, the bedroom door opened. "Hey, you okay? I heard a noise."

My stepsister, Dawn, stood in the doorway, her highlighted hair tied back into a neat swirl, her face like a teen magazine cover model's even without makeup. Her body always appeared flawlessly curvy, even now when it was covered with a giant Tweety T-shirt. I had no idea how she did it.

Getting a good look at me sprawled on the floor, Dawn's

eyes grew wide. "Dude," she said, "wow. You look . . . wow."

I got to my feet, trying to ignore the stunned look on her face.

Then she took in the open window, the pale yellow curtains fluttering in the evening breeze. "Going somewhere?" she asked.

I hesitated, because I didn't understand what I'd been doing. The way I'd been thinking . . . wanting to leap outside and run around? Not wanting to pick up a call from Megan, of all people? It didn't make sense. I would never do that.

I stood, shivering. The breeze was insanely cold. I shoved the window down and latched it.

Dawn shut the door and came to my side. "Hey, you didn't hit your head or anything, did you?" She crouched down and set the desk chair upright, eyes not leaving my face. "It would suck if you just learned how to dress less like a soccer mom only to have to miss out on the first day of school because of a concussion."

"No," I muttered. "No, I'm okay, I think, it's just . . . Emily's dead."

"Is that a metaphor or something? Like the old Emily is dead and this"—Dawn waved her hand at my clothes—"is the new Emily? That's so meta."

It took a moment for me to realize what Dawn

meant—then I glanced down and saw my cleavage. My very exposed cleavage. I spun toward the mirror that hung next to the open closet and saw myself: short-shorts, way-too-small shirt, brown hair flowing to my shoulders, no glasses, and way too much makeup—vampy red lips and smoky eyes, like I was about to head out to go clock in for my shift at the local house of ill repute.

"Oh, what the—" My arms shot up to cover my chest. "I look—I don't know what—"

I never dressed like that. Ever. The day I sprouted breasts and hips before all the other girls in my grade was the day I learned what it felt like to have everyone stare at me, not knowing what they were thinking. Wondering if they thought my lumps and bulges were as hideous as I did, feeling ashamed as other kids pointed, snickered behind their palms, brushed their hands against parts they shouldn't have gone near.

So, yeah, my attire generally didn't include cleavage.

I met Dawn's confused eyes, tried to pretend I wasn't embarrassed that she was seeing me like this. "I opened the window and Megan called. She was checking on me because another girl named Emily was found. Dead, I mean. She was shot not all that far from here."

"Oh no," Dawn said. She sat on my bed and picked up the plush Corgi dog that sat at its end, cradling it in her lap.

"That's so sad. And really scary. Did you know her?"

"No, not really," I said. "She was Emily C. and I was Emily W., in every class ever, but that was about it. We aren't—weren't—into the same things."

Dawn held up the stuffed toy dog. "So she wouldn't have any Corgis named Ein, then?"

"She was more into clothes and stuff, I think." I shook my head. "I can't believe it. Emily Cooke . . ."

"That's so sad," Dawn said again. She stood, arranging Ein just so on my wrinkled bedspread and gave me a serious look. "But if someone just got shot down the street, going outside right now is not a good idea, Em. Whoever did it could still be out there."

"Yeah, no outside for me. I don't even like outside. I don't know what . . ." I trailed off as I went back to studying myself. Whatever feeling that had possessed me to start climbing out my freakin' second-story *window* was long gone, and now I was feeling . . . normal again.

I went to my closet. Digging through the dirty laundry piled on the floor, I found the ratty University of Washington hoodie I usually wore around the house and pulled it on. All covered up, like I preferred. Surveying myself in the mirror, I said, "There."

"Seriously, Emily, middle ground," Dawn said as she came up behind me. "You don't need to go over the top, but you are way too good-looking to hide yourself under a hoodie. Boys are only gonna see you as one of the guys if you dress like this all the time."

I pulled my hair back into a ponytail. "Thanks, but that's just not me. I don't mind that boys don't see me as anything."

It was a lie. Of course I hoped that maybe one day someone would notice me, even if I was afraid of what they'd think when they did. But admitting that to Dawn would have given her way too much ammo to fire the next time she tried to convince me to let her do a makeover.

Dawn threw her hands up, surrendering. "Okay, well, don't say I didn't try to share my older-stepsister wisdom. I just want you to discover the inherent hotness that is Emily Webb before it's too late."

I turned Dawn toward the bedroom door and playfully pushed her out. "All righty, fashion hour extravaganza is over, I need to go to bed now. First day of school tomorrow."

"No going out your window!" Dawn said as she began to close the door.

I kicked off my sandals. "I won't. I wasn't really going to go outside, I was just hot."

Dawn gave me a doubtful look.

"Hey," I said. "I was gonna ask you, this weekend sometime: you, me, and a Whedonverse marathon? I feel a need to get my Buffy on."

"'Get my Buffy on'?" Dawn shook her head. "Seriously? Once we rid you of your shlubby clothes, we've really got to work on how you talk."

"What's wrong with how I talk?"

"Too large a topic to deal with now, Grasshopper." Dawn pointed at me. "Now, wait. Don't think changing the subject will make me forget about the window thing. Seriously, there could be some wacko out there killing people."

"Don't worry, I got it. No sneaking out."

I smiled at Dawn as she gave me a flippy wave and headed to her room, then shut my bedroom door and leaned back against it to take in a long, deep breath.

Okay, so whoa. Let's stop for a second, flip it, and reverse it, because listen: As you've likely guessed by now, I was so not the type of girl who gets dressed up in tight clothes and sneaks out of windows. I'd never snuck out of anything in my life. I didn't have any place to sneak out to. My idea of a fun night was diving into the massive To Be Read pile of books stacked near my dresser, or draping myself in a Slanket and marathoning old sci-fi shows on DVD. No latest fashions, no parties, no football games—I was the girl with the big sweatshirts who loved everything geeky.

What I wasn't was someone who ran around dressed like she just got finished with a particularly sleazy *Maxim* photo shoot. Maybe that was what the other Emily was like, but I don't know. I guess I'll never know.

Yet only a few minutes before, I'd felt . . . different. Wild, free from all my debilitating self-consciousness, and, well, pretty. It had been thrilling, because I can't lie—I'd thought about it. A lot. What it would feel like to not be so endlessly mousy, not so ashamed of what I hid beneath baggy clothes. To instead be a girl who oozed confidence, who was actually at ease with the body she was stuck in. Someone graceful and commanding and as kick-ass as the women in all the books and shows and movies I loved.

But still. You usually don't just *become* that type of girl overnight. It was all massively unsettling.

I opened my top dresser drawer. Pulling a makeup wipe from its little box, I began to clean my face. I had to really scrub. The makeup was heavy and thick, foundation cracking on my cheeks and the eyeliner goopy. The chemical in the wipe stung my eyes and made my contacts burn.

I went to the bathroom and popped them out. My reflected image went blurry around the edges, and I remembered how the book on my floor had seemed fuzzy while I was talking to Megan, even with my contacts in. Then Megan had told me about Emily Cooke, my brain had gone all dizzy, and I'd started to see clearly again just as I began to feel normal.

Yeah. That was weird.

I finished wiping off the makeup, put on my glasses, and examined my reflection. Except for the short-shorts, I looked like myself again.

I studied my face beyond the toothpaste-splattered mirror. "What were you going to do?" I asked my reflection. "You're not going all Jekyll and Hyde, are you?"

Biting my lip, I thought about what had happened. All I remembered was sitting on my bed, resting against the headboard, reading my book, and then . . . Everything between that moment and the phone call from Megan was a blur.

My bedroom had felt so tiny, so stuffy, and outside had seemed so open, so wide and breezy and interesting, that I had to go out there and . . . do what, exactly?

"What were you going to do?" I asked myself.

My reflection stood there silent, as clueless as I was.

2

I MEAN, IT COULD HAVE BEEN ME

By the next morning I'd completely forgotten about Emily Cooke. Having a close encounter with an alternate personality tends to weigh on your mind, and that was on top of the whole first-day-of-school thing.

Megan picked me up in her old rust bucket of a car. She cursed the whole way to school—about her car, other cars on the road, old people crossing the road, the glare from the rising sun, the nasally voice of the DJ on the radio—on and on.

Megan's not exactly a morning person.

School picked up with the same routine as every year. Megan stormed through the halls in her black skinny jeans and black dress-tunic thing and black sunglasses, her butt-length blond hair slapping me in the side as she whipped her head around to meet everyone's eyes, daring them to say something. Meanwhile I sort of shuffled alongside her, folded in on myself, my eyes not leaving the schedule I held. Every now and then I'd glance up from the green tile floors to make sure I wasn't going to walk into someone or something, but otherwise I did my very best to stand in Megan's shadow and let her be angry enough at the world for the both of us.

This year Megan and I shared the same homeroom: Ms. Nguyen, our calculus teacher by day/local access Vietnamese talk show host by night. I sat at a desk halfway back, by the windows, with Megan beside me. Everyone else in the class was loud and laughing: The girls with their camis and tight jeans and glossy hair were huddled in little groups getting all *ohmigod* about something, the guys acting like complete jackasses as usual. They were straight out of The CW Land, a magical place where everyone dates everyone else, then gets all dramatic about it. A land of excitement and wonder where everybody spoke a language I had no hope of understanding.

Of course, there were other "geeks" scattered about— some tiny girl in the front with curly hair and wire-frame glasses who shivered like she was cold, a chubby guy near the door wearing an unfortunately patterned button-up shirt and sporting the skeezy little mustache boys get. And Megan, eyes aimed at the ceiling, arms crossed, letting out pointed sighs to show how over everything she was.

Only, they weren't like me, not really. Because geeky can be worked if you know how to pull it off. You like things not in the mainstream? There's definitely a group you can click with somewhere in school—I'm pretty sure I've seen glasses girl and mustache guy in the same after-school LARP club.

But here's the thing about me and school: I didn't fit into any of those neat cliques, because I didn't know how to make myself fit. Among all the kids in our little suburban school— the freaks and the nerds, the jocks and the cheerleaders—I was hopelessly apart. Just me, Emily Webb, alone, counting the hours until school was done and I got to go back home to my room and my DVDs and my books.

My only real friend was Megan. She could be dour, yeah, but I didn't blame her, not really. Back in junior high, she'd spent three years trying desperately to join the in crowd, though her overly eager efforts were met mostly by whispered mocking in the halls and the occasional harassing email.

I stuck by her through it all, halfheartedly helping her with her plans to be cool despite not having any idea what cool was. One of the girls, Sarah Plainsworth, the ringleader of what could best be called a tween *Mean Girls*, actually seemed to take pity on Megan one day. She introduced Megan to a boy from another school—online, of course—and set about arranging a date for them. Megan was more excited than I'd ever seen her, and we'd spent a week finding her the perfect outfit, and the perfect hair, and practicing the perfect things to say.

Only, of course, there was no boy. The date had Megan standing alone in a family-style Japanese restaurant as Sarah and those she'd wrangled in on the gag sat around a hibachi table and laughed. Megan had stood there, shaking, focusing on the chefs making little volcanoes out of onion slices to keep from seeing the faces of those mocking her.

Something clicked then. She finally got that, for whatever reason, people like Sarah Plainsworth would never let her become a part of their seemingly perfect lives. And so Megan just looked Sarah square in the eye until the girl no longer laughed, then left, leaving those kids and her dreams of being somebody like them behind.

Sarah Plainsworth moved away between junior high and high school, and with her left the memories of her epic prank—for everyone except Megan. Freshman year, Megan came back to school all withering attitude and black clothes. A whole new girl.

I watched Megan glare at a shiny blond girl sitting near her, and it made me wonder what she'd think if she knew about my alter ego the night before. About my weird, temporary mood swing. Because if there was one thing I knew about Megan, it was that she trusted me to always be me. Quiet and with an ear only for her. Not someone who dressed flashy or trashy, not someone who longed to go out on the town to mingle with people very much like bitchy party girl Sarah Plainsworth.

I stooped over my desk and ran my finger over a name carved into the faux-wood top, still trying and failing to recall everything that had happened between reading and Megan's phone call. Maybe, for just a moment, I'd managed to flip the normal teen switch in my head. Maybe, for just a moment, whatever issues made me so hopelessly incapable of fitting in with anyone had gone away. Megan wouldn't like it, not at all. But maybe if I figured it all out, then we could figure her out too.

I didn't get the chance to think about it further, because the second bell rang and Ms. Nguyen swished into class.

"Good morning!" Her voice was loud, her smile broad and bleached. She sounded exactly like you'd expect a local access talk show host slumming as a high school teacher to sound. She was never boring, Ms. Nguyen. Today she wore a canary yellow pantsuit accessorized with a red and purple scarf tied round her neck, and her hair was shellacked into a bob last seen in 1967.

I sort of loved her.

"Another year is upon us," Ms. Nguyen announced as she sat in a chair, crossed her legs, and cradled a cup of coffee in her lap. She took a sip, then made a face. "Oh, that is just terrible."

I laughed a little too loudly and got a wink from the short guy sitting in front of Megan. Spencer Holt was the sort of goofy guy who was just funny enough to get to hang out with all the cool kids as their token comedian. I'd seen him around for years, but had never really talked to him. He grinned over at me, and, heat rushing to my cheeks, I looked down at my desk.

Ms. Nguyen set the coffee cup on her desk and was about to resume speaking when the door opened. A small woman with a somber face stood there, and she beckoned Ms. Nguyen over. They huddled together and spoke in hushed tones in the hallway while the whole class watched.

Megan sighed. "Let's get on with it already," she muttered.

When Ms. Nguyen came back a moment later, she seemed a different person. She sat back in her chair at the front of the class, hands trembling.

"Ms. Nguyen?" A pretty, redheaded girl in the back stood up, concerned. Nikki Tate, the head cheerleader.

Ms. Nguyen shook her head and looked over the class

as though she was just now seeing us. Her eyes welled up with tears.

Something inside my chest twisted, like a spring wound too tight. Something horrible had happened . . . and it was then that I remembered, and I felt like a total jerk for forgetting: Emily Cooke had died last night. Emily Cooke had died, and no one knew except me and Megan. And now everyone who knew her—who actually knew her, not like me—would hear about it, and . . .

I hunched over my desk, eyes down. I didn't want to see anyone's face. I felt strangely guilty, because I'd known about this horrible secret and should have said something. Ms. Nguyen spoke, her voice quiet and shaky, but I didn't really hear her words, just the sadness in them. She told us that a student had been found murdered the night before and that we were going to have an assembly about it later. The class listened in shocked silence.

"Who is it?" the guy behind me asked. "Who died?"

Shoving my glasses up my nose with my index finger, I dared a glance up at Ms. Nguyen. She seemed to wobble in place before blinking and taking us all in. It was as though she'd mentally drifted off somewhere and only now realized she wasn't alone. "I know many of you were her friends," Ms. Nguyen said. "She was a lovely girl, a lovely girl. . . ."

"Who?" Nikki Tate whispered from her seat in the back. "Please tell us."

Ms. Nguyen's face contorted in grief. "Emily," she finally said. "It's Emily Cooke." And Ms. Nguyen began to sob.

The air felt sucked out of the room.

A chair squealed as it was hastily shoved back, and a girl ran past. I only saw her for a second before she tore open the classroom door and was in the hallway—Mai Sato, a big track star around school. Only then did I remember that she and Emily Cooke were friends.

Mai's flight set the room buzzing with whispered chatter. Normally Ms. Nguyen would have put a stop to that, but she was softly crying to herself in her seat while Nikki Tate and the curly-haired girl from up front comforted her. I never knew Ms. Nguyen cared so much about Emily Cooke. But then again, I didn't really know anything about Emily Cooke, did I?

Beside me, Megan stared at the ceiling, completely unfazed. Listening to the crying of the shiny blond girl next to her, she rolled her eyes.

"Drama queens," she muttered in my direction.

The assembly that closed the first day of school wasn't the usual kind; even the rowdiest of the boys kept it down in respect as the principal and a woman from the police department spoke to all of us. They stood on the Carver High Cougars mascot painted in the center of the basketball court and took turns at the microphone. They said very little about the details of the murder but made it clear that they were concerned about student safety in light of the incident—seeing as how Emily Cooke was killed while alone on the streets of a good neighborhood—and that everyone should go straight home from school.

I sat next to Megan in the top row of the bleachers, listening as precautions were discussed. We were told to always keep in groups of twos or threes, and to get rides from trusted friends or family instead of walking. Megan picked absently at the plastic bench as she stared at the ceiling, but I couldn't help watching the kids around me. There were more than a few who hugged one another and cried openly, even some guys. It felt surreal, like something out of a movie. I half expected somber music to play over the scene while a camera zoomed in on my pointedly thoughtful expression.

As the school officials droned on, Megan slipped on her sunglasses and scowled in the direction of four girls huddled together, mascara tears drawing black lines down their cheeks. They held one another and whispered what I guessed were comforting words, their faces ugly in their grief.

"'Oh, *wah*,'" Megan mimicked as she watched the girls. "'Emily Cooke and I were, like, totally best friends. Like, we used to go shopping all the time, and we shared a boyfriend that one time. Now who will tell me which shade of pink goes best with my lip liner? Death is so not fair.'"

"Megan . . . ," I whispered.

She ignored me. "They should just tell everyone what really happened. That Emily C. decided to walk barefoot for three miles in her pajamas. Did I tell you her parents caught her acting all dazed and out of it earlier that week too? So don't take an evening stroll dressed for bed and cracked out on drugs, and bam, you won't be murdered."

"Megan, come on. A girl is dead."

Megan peered at me over her sunglasses. "Okay, you are, like, the Queen of Schlocky Horror Flicks. I have no idea why you're so mopey. Why does this bother you so much?"

"Those are movies," I said. "This is real life. It's different. I mean, it could have been me."

Megan frowned. "What? Why would it have been you? 'Cause you're both named Emily?" She flicked her hand dismissively. "That's stupid. It's not like you're dumb enough to wander blazed into dark neighborhoods like Emily C."

I remembered the open window, my outstretched leg,

the darkness that had seemed so inviting. I remembered my own freaky—though not drug-fueled—mind lapse.

"Yeah," I said. "I'd never do that."

We watched as the class president, Tracie Townsend, took the floor to give a hastily written eulogy. "Anyway," Megan said, talking over her, "you hate these girls as much as I do. Give it a week, no one will even remember what Emily C. looked like, I guarantee you."

"You didn't seem to think that way last night when you were worried it was me," I said.

"Well, that would be different. You actually matter."

Harsh. But that was Megan. I was used to it. But I also didn't have anything to say in response.

We fell silent as Tracie began speaking in that curt way of hers, her pretty features turned down in a frown, and her perfect black curls bobbing with her somber nods. I considered telling Megan that, no, I didn't actually *hate* any of the other girls at school. Though some had gone out of their way to make Megan's life hell, they never really did anything to me. And anyway, even though Megan wasn't exactly the forgive-and-forget type, as far as I was concerned all of that was over the day Sarah Plainsworth left. Now no one really seemed to care one way or the other about us.

I also considered telling Megan about what had happened the night before—the clothes, the window, all of it.

But no, I couldn't admit any of that. Anything that would make Megan think I was going to get all glossy and popular would not go over well. Even if most girls wouldn't consider my idea of dressing to be "glossy and popular" so much as "sleazy and desperate." I didn't think Megan would make the distinction. Not after she'd had us make a pact never to become like "them."

Besides, it was just a one-time freaky mental slip.

Or was it? Maybe it wasn't drugs that had made the other Emily seem so weird to her parents. Maybe there was something going around, some sort of personality-altering disease. I mean, what would possess Emily Cooke to go wandering miles from her house, barefoot and wearing only her pajamas, especially on the same night I dressed like a streetwalker and decided to jump out my window?

Maybe it was the weirdness of the night before, or the bizarreness of coping with an entire school filled with shocked people walking around like zombies all day, but I didn't *feel* right. Something felt shifted inside of me, off center and wobbly, and no matter how hard I tried I couldn't put that unnameable something back in place.

Megan nudged me as Tracie finished speaking and the kids in the bleachers applauded politely. "Hey, don't get all silent on me," she whispered. "It sucks that the other Emily got whacked, okay?"

24

I opened my mouth to speak, but I didn't get a word out before a girl turned around and shushed us. Embarrassed, I clamped my lips closed. Megan rolled her eyes but didn't say anything.

We sat there, silent, as the rest of the world's most depressing assembly death-marched to its somber finish and we could finally go home, where I could escape into a book and forget all about dead teenagers and strange mood swings and this horrible sensation that after last night, nothing was quite right anymore in our school or our small town.

BIG OL' FATTY HAMBEAST

Nothing gets your mind off of depressing thoughts of dead teenagers like being called fat on the internet.

It happened the same day as the assembly. Nothing was on TV that night—it was only early September, after all, and new TV seasons don't start until mid-month—so I was in my room. I'd come home from the horrible downer of school five hours earlier after riding alongside Megan through a torrent of rain that fogged up her windows, the world outside hidden behind a gray mist. I'd say that the weather had matched the day's downcast mood, but I knew that was a joke. The writhing storm clouds would soon give way to blue skies before returning a few hours later along with, like, a flurry of hail or something. No one's mood is as bipolar as western Washington weather.

After racing through the downpour to my front door, I hugged my dad, where he sat at his desk killing undead hordes in his computer game, then decided I'd distract myself by trying once again to read *Lord of the Rings*, since it felt like my geeky duty to do so. I didn't last long at that— yes, I know, I should feel horribly ashamed that I can't get past all the hobbit singing to get into the story. Instead I went browsing online.

Maybe it's just me, but hearing about someone my own age, someone I vaguely knew, dying . . . it wouldn't leave me alone. Forget my giant DVD case filled with movies about teenagers getting murdered—I'd seen so much CGI and makeup and red-dyed corn syrup that when it came to the idea of another teenager dying it never seemed real. I'd never really considered that one day I could walk outside and get shot, and it would be all over.

So maybe that's why I Googled "Emily Cooke" and spent hours reading about her. There were local news articles about the mysterious murder, of course, and a whole slew of blog posts from people who'd known her, talking about their shock. Some people posted letters of hers they'd saved—surprisingly well-written letters that contained amusing haikus and clever, off-kilter short stories about the person she had written to.

Eventually I ended up on Emily Cooke's own blog. I clicked through the pictures of her smiling with her friends, then started to read all the comments from people saying how much they'd miss her.

In the middle of those comments, I saw this:

Terrizzle Sept 8, 4:54 p.m.
sad ur dead emily ur much hoter than fat Emily

My first thought: *"Terrizzle" (real name Terrance Sedgwick) should not be in eleventh grade and writing like that.* Capitalization, punctuation, and spelling words out aren't that difficult, especially in what's supposed to be a message to a dearly departed friend . . . or a hot girl he wanted to hook up with, whatever.

My second thought: *Wait, "fat Emily"?* There are—or, well, were—only two Emilys in our class, which meant . . .

Oh. Oh no.

Here's a fun fact about me: Like the partial truth I'd told Dawn the night before, the last thing I ever wanted was for guys like Terrance to look at, think about, or talk about me to other people. The mere idea was completely terrifying. Even so, I guess I had always sort of fantasized that a guy would see me and get past the ponytail and the glasses and the giant sweatshirt to discover how insanely awesome I am, then come and whisk me off into that magical teenager fairyland where everyone else gets to prance around.

But nope. A guy, some random guy at school, looked at me and thought, *What a heifer. What a pig.* And then wished, if anyone named Emily had to die, that it had been me. The "fat" one. That way he could continue to think about Emily Cooke's hotness without having to feel weird about how she's now lying on a cold slab in a morgue somewhere.

I blinked and stared at the screen some more, feeling like there were crowds of pretty teenagers standing in my room and ogling me, judging me. I could almost see long gone Sarah Plainsworth giving me that withering glare of hers. My cheeks burned, and though I didn't really believe the words I was about to say, I whispered to myself, "I'm not fat."

It didn't matter what I said to myself, though, because I knew this to be true: All that mattered was how others perceived you. If others saw me and thought, *Big ol' fatty hambeast*, then that's who I was. And now everyone at school would see this and know all about what Terrance Sedgwick thought of previously invisible me.

The clock ticked away on my computer from 8:07 to 8:11 and still I couldn't stop from sitting there, staring at my computer screen and feeling utterly embarrassed by that one stupid comment.

And then, at 8:14, my guts twisted and I gasped.

A massive shudder ran through my body, as though the ground was quaking beneath me, and I fell out of my chair onto the floor. I clutched my stomach, clenched my teeth, and felt my toes curl. Another twist inside my gut and I dry heaved, but my stomach was unwilling to release whatever poisons I was sure were swirling inside of me.

I tried to call out, but the only sound I could make was a pitiful squeak. Not that anyone would hear me if I did yell, anyway—my dad was downstairs with his headphones turned up while he played his game, and my stepmom and Dawn were out. Whatever this was—a seizure?—wasn't stopping, and I couldn't breathe, and I couldn't move, and no one could help me, and oh God was I going to die?

And then, as the red digital numbers on my nightstand alarm clock switched to 8:15, it was over.

I felt . . . different.

I felt *good*.

I lay on the floor, my breathing calming as my heart slowed from a frantic pounding to steady, confident thumps. I arched my back and stretched my arms above my head, cricking my neck as I did. My entire body felt stiff, atrophied from lack of any appreciable amount of movement. This wouldn't do at all.

I grabbed the edge of my desk and pulled myself to my feet. Emily Cooke's blog was still open on my computer screen, Terrizzle's message of my fatness front and center. I read it again.

And I laughed.

"Oh, please," I said aloud. Seriously, Terrance of all people should not be calling people fat. The boy wasn't exactly svelte himself.

I turned to my right and caught my reflection in the mirror. The image was blurry even with my glasses on, so I squinted to see better. Hoodie two sizes too large? Check. Completely plain face and hair? Double check. No wonder Terrizzle thought I was a fatty.

But I could show him, couldn't I? If bad teen romantic comedies taught me anything, it's that glasses-and-ponytail girls are always in need of emergency makeovers. So I snapped the glasses off my face and let my hair down. Without the glasses I didn't need to squint anymore—I could see fine. And though that shouldn't have made any sense, at that moment all I thought was: *Wicked.*

I tilted my head. Better, but not quite right. I tore off the oppressive hoodie and T-shirt I'd had on underneath, then studied my torso, clad only in an old-lady bra my step-mom had bought me. My hips and chest? Sure, they were wider than some other girls', but in a definite old-school, busty-pinup-girl sort of way. But my waist was more or less narrow, in no way fat unless your idea of fat was anyone above a size zero, in which case you needed your head examined.

Ten minutes later, I regarded myself in the mirror again. I'd raided the part of Dawn's closet dedicated to her clubbing clothes and had a brand-new look: a slinky, sparkly, and backless gold shirt that accentuated my décolletage, a black miniskirt, and some tall, black, spiky-heeled boots. With a pair of dangly gold hoop earrings to finish the ensemble and my eyes and lips done, I looked like Dawn normally does when she's ready to hit the clubs. Which is to say, less comically sleazy than I'd looked the night before.

I was definitely stepping up my game and was well outside the realm of "chaste." The main goal was to look like some fat teen guy's late-night fantasy. Perfect for how I planned to mess with Terrance's head.

I opened the bedroom door, then hesitated—I could probably slip past my dad, engrossed as he was in his video game. When his construction jobs slowed down like they always did this time of year, my dad spent all his free time playing online role-playing games. He was oblivious during the best of his endless days of online gaming, but I didn't want to chance it.

So I turned to my window. It was dark outside, but there

was a depth to the darkness that I needed to explore. I raised the window. The rain had petered out sometime during the evening. A cool fall breeze rushed into my room and blew back my hair, smelling of damp leaves and excitement.

As with the night before, I used my desk chair to boost myself up, then stepped one foot out the window. Unlike the night before, no one called me, no one barged into my room to see if I was okay.

I ducked my torso through the window, then my other leg, and balanced on the windowsill. Clouds billowed above in a moonless sky, and the glistening road beneath me was empty. I could hear the neighbor kids next door watching something on TV.

With a quick breath, I placed my heeled boots against the siding of the house, tensed my arms to push myself free, and leaped.

For a few elated seconds, I flew through the air, weightless and hollow and completely fearless. I sensed the ground approaching before I saw it, and as I arced down I pulled my body into a crouch and positioned my feet in preparation.

I landed perfectly, silently. On spiky heels. On a sidewalk about thirty feet away and twenty feet down from my bedroom window.

You know what I realize now? Of course the leap was something clearly not in the remote realm of possibility for normal, average, everyday Emily Webb. But on that night, with the adrenaline pumping and excitement skittering across my skin, I didn't thinking anything of it, as though leaping from my second-story window was something I did every time I felt like going out.

I slowly stood. Making sure my top and skirt were straight, and my hair still in place, I turned east down the empty road. Terrizzle's house was that way. I knew because Megan lived near him, and we'd of course seen each other around the neighborhood. Which was probably how he knew about me in the first place, seeing as how we didn't have any classes together.

I stood on the sidewalk beneath the flickering street-light and thought, *The only thing better than embarrassing Terrance would be embarrassing him in front of a witness.*

So, first stop: Megan's house.

Stop after that: Terrizzle's place.

After that: Who knew? I had hours to go before morning. And I intended to have as much fun as those few hours would allow.

Satisfied and unable to stop grinning, I strode down the street, determined to own the night.

WHAT AM I?

I intended to go straight to Megan's house. Really, I did. But as I strutted down the street that first night, distractions surrounded me. Around me, houses were dark under the black sky, shrouded in the shadows of the towering evergreens that rose toward the starry night. From each house, yellow light glowed through curtains and blue light shimmered from TVs.

I could feel the snapping of the electricity coursing through the power lines over my head. It sizzled against my skin as I walked beneath the streetlamps, making the fine hair on my arms bristle. I stopped in the sulfurous glow of one streetlamp, closed my eyes, and spread my arms, taking it in. It reminded me of the one and only time Megan and I had gone to a tanning salon.

Megan. Right. I was on a mission.

Back to business, I lowered my arms and moved on. A few of my neighbors' front lawns were overmanicured, choked with carefully tended trees and rosebushes. Overwhelming the scents of wet grass, leaves, and flowers was the thick stench of an animal farm along with some sort of sharp chemical odor. Whatever manure these people were using was totally nauseating.

A car horn blared, and headlights blinded me. I shielded my eyes as brakes squealed, felt a rush of air as a bumper came barreling toward me. I leaped back as the car jerked to a stop, an inch away from hitting me. Only then did I realize I'd left the sidewalk and had been standing in the middle of the road, driven there by the stink of all the fertilizer and chemicals.

The car that had almost hit me was boxy, its engine loud and grumbling. A total junker. The guy in the driver's seat leaned out his window and threw his hand in the air.

"Get out of the road!" he shouted. "Stupid bitch!"

What did he just call me?

I lowered my arm slowly. The guy's hair was greasy and long, his eyes rimmed red.

I didn't move. "I'm not stupid, and I don't respond well to name-calling," I said. "Say it again and see what happens."

Cursing, the guy pressed on the gas and the car roared. Exhaust, tinted red from his taillights, billowed out the back. Tires screeched as he lurched forward, right toward me. He apparently wasn't bothering to swerve.

I stepped calmly back toward the sidewalk, a rush of wind blowing back my hair as he zoomed past. We could have left it at that. But before the guy passed all the way, he reached his left hand out his window and threw something over the roof of his car. Right at me.

My hand shot into the sky before I'd even realized I was about to be smacked in the face. I lowered my hand to discover that I had snatched an oversize plastic Taco Bell cup out of the air. Watered-down soda and half-melted ice clinked inside.

The guy had thrown his drink at me.

Well, now, he shouldn't have done that. Name-calling, trying to run me down? I could maybe forgive that—I *had* been standing in the middle of the road, after all. But throwing things was totally uncalled for.

I gripped the cup tightly, plastic crumpling, and sprang forward. Arms pumping and sticky soda spilling out of the cup, I raced down the street, my heels clacking against the asphalt.

The guy's brakes complained as he paused at the end of the street at the stop sign. So what if he threw drinks at teen girls walking on the street? At least he obeyed basic traffic laws.

What a guy.

I stopped right next to his window, breathing easily despite how fast I'd dashed. The guy was checking the road to the right, didn't even see me—until he turned his head left to make sure it was safe to go. Then he jumped back in his seat, startled.

"What—," he sputtered.

"You dropped something," I said.

I lobbed the Taco Bell cup into the car. It smacked his chest, hard, and syrupy brown liquid splattered his windshield and across his shirt. I jumped back to avoid being splashed.

Jaw tensed, the guy fumbled with his seat belt and the car door at the same time. "What the f—!" he started to scream.

I laughed wildly, totally exhilarated. Someone messed with me, I got even—a concept that before today had been totally foreign to me. Totally foreign to simpering daytime me, that is, who reacted to any sort of aggression by ducking her head, apologizing, then hiding in her room until it all blew over.

This was *so* much more fun.

Before the guy could finish getting out of his car, I

turned and ran north down the street, feeling like I was flying. Even in heels, I made each bounding step with ease, some part of me just *knowing* how to move like an Olympic athlete. I heard the guy following, ranting and raving, his footsteps plodding. He gasped for breath after only a brief chase, and I felt a little disappointed—there was no way this guy could keep up with me. How boring.

So I slowed down, turned around, and jogged backward. He lumbered forward, soda dripping from the ends of his stringy hair. Behind him, his car sat running in the street, the driver's-side door wide open.

"Come on!" I called. "Are you really gonna lose a race to a girl in a miniskirt and heels? I mean, really."

"You're . . . you're crazy!" he gasped as he drew close. "I'll—"

"You'll what? Pass out after making another few insults? Is your plan to beat me down with that barbed wit of yours? Or do you have more trash to throw at me?"

I stopped altogether and put my hands on my hips. The guy—completely out of shape despite being stick thin—stumbled toward me, panting.

Then anger surged over his face. His muscles tensed—first his jaw, then his arms, then legs—and I knew, I just *knew*, that in two more steps he'd leap at me.

So when he did, I simply stepped to the side. The guy

barreled forward, grasping at nothing. He tripped over his feet and fell to his knees, landing with a crack against the wet sidewalk. Hissing in pain, he rolled onto his side.

I stood over him. "I'm tired of playing," I said. "If you see me again, just drive around."

With that, I turned and sauntered between a row of hedges into someone's dark backyard, leaving the stoner behind me.

I stopped, taking in my surroundings. The porch light was off, but I could make out a partially inflated kiddie pool by the sliding glass doors. Inside it, brown leaves and evergreen needles floated atop stagnant rainwater. Next to the kiddie pool there were a few dirty, cracked plastic lawn chairs. The rest of the backyard—the grassy area— appeared to be empty.

I started to hike across the backyard when a thought hit me.

What am I?

It seemed a useless thought, coming from the daytime part of my brain that I wished would stay hidden. What was I? I was Emily Webb. I was hot, and I was smart, and I was quick enough to chase down cars on a whim. Duh.

And I had a mission. I needed to get dominant. I needed to find someone like me, someone better than average, someone agile and intelligent, someone who smelled *right*.

I needed to be away from the stifling world of manicured lawns and blaring TVs and kiddie pools—needed to be under a canopy of trees, preparing.

"Wait," I said aloud. "What?"

I squeezed my eyes shut and shoved back the out-of-place desires and daytime me's questioning voice. It didn't matter what Daytime Emily had to say about the weird urges. My mission was to find Megan, then find Terrance, then do something to get back at him.

Ready to get back to the business of vengeance, I continued across the lawn, toward the back fence. As I did, something barked to my left.

It was a small, curly-haired dog, standing in front of a doghouse I hadn't seen in the darkness of the backyard. It flattened back its ears and growled.

I turned to the dog, considering it. Then I lunged forward and spread out my arms, like a bully psyching out a little kid on a playground. The dog yelped, tucked its tail between its legs, and darted inside its house.

I straightened back up and laughed.

From now on this would be me, I decided. No more hiding in plain sight. No more taking trash talk from anyone—especially not from yappy little dogs. No more being afraid to speak my mind. My usual self spent so much time worrying about how others would perceive her that she never actually *did* anything. What kind of life was that?

I knew it deep down in my bones: I was a new Emily Webb. And this new Emily Webb was better than the old one in every way imaginable. Was even better than the Emily I'd wanted to be back in junior high.

I reached the back of the yard, sidled between two trees, coiled my legs, and prepared to leap over the fence. But then I stopped. Suddenly I felt as though someone was close, watching me. So close that it made the tiny hairs on my arms stand on end.

Thinking it was the cracked-out driver guy following me, or maybe even that dog, I spun on my heels to face whoever was behind me.

No one was there.

Except I could still feel someone, some *thing*, looking at me. Even though the yard was empty. Even though no curtains moved at the back of the house in front of me.

Now I realize I should have paid more attention to that sensation. But then, at that moment, I grew quickly bored and brushed away the feeling. I turned away from the yard and leaped over the six-foot fence as if doing so was perfectly normal.

I continued north, shutting out all the distractions—voices seeping out of walls, cars pulling into and out of driveways, animals cawing and barking and mewling. I passed the small library that looked more like someone's house than a place to check out books—the midpoint between my house and Megan's. The homes went from being mostly two stories with big yards to mostly one story and cramped together.

Megan's house stood dark at the end of the street. All the windows that I could see were shadowed, and though Megan's car was parked at the curb in front of her small lawn, her parents' cars were gone.

Perfect. No nosy adults getting in my way.

I strode across the street and headed around the side of the garage to Megan's window. It was closed and the curtains drawn, but I could see her shadow moving in the orange glow of her desk lamp.

My plan was to crouch in the bushes beneath her window, slam my hand against the glass, and freak her out. But that changed when I heard the strains of a guitar being tuned and the thumping of drums. The garage.

Hmm. Scare Megan or go see what her brother was doing with his band? Angry Megan, or boys playing rock and roll?

Really, there was no question.

The Vesper Company
"Envisioning the brightest stars, to lead our way."
- Internal Document, Do Not Reproduce -

Partial Transcript of the Interrogation of
Branch B's Vesper 1
Part 2—Recorded Oct. 31, 2010

F. Savage (FS): Hmm. Make a note: The nature of
the—
Vesper 1 (V1): Make a note?
FS: Ah, sorry, I'm just making a statement aloud
for the record. So I can refer back to the tran-
script when writing my full report.
V1: Got it. Sorry.
FS: Make a note: The nature and actions of these
deviants—
V1: Deviants?
FS: Excuse me?
V1: You people call us deviants?
FS: I'm afraid that "deviants" is the slang term
that we came up with in-house for those of you
we haven't . . . observed. I assure you it is not
meant as a suggestion of your character.

V1: [laughs.] It's actually quite appropriate, so, whatever.

FS: [clears throat.] As I was saying, the nature of these deviants, as suggested by the actions of Vesper 1—

V1: Wait, so which is it? Am I a vesper or a deviant?

FS: Emily, *please*. We're on a schedule. [V1 begins to speak; FS talks over her.] The nature of these *deviants*, as suggested by Vesper 1's actions during the events detailed in chapters three and four of her written account, would indicate that they develop heightened abilities based on some sort of time schedule. One that also alters their personalities before they—

V1: Turn into even more of a deviant.

FS: Excuse me? Uh, no, no, I meant before you— [Distant, thumping noises echo; FS and V1 fall silent for several moments. Distant noises fall silent.]

V1: That normal around here?

FS: Ah, not particularly. Usually quite silent. I haven't . . . I think we should continue on with your account.

V1: Aren't you going to finish dictating your note to self?

FS: [sighs.] Forget it. Let's just move on.

THE BUBONIC TEUTONICS

The garage's side door was unlocked, so I didn't bother knocking. Megan's older brother Lucas was there with a long white guitar hanging from his shoulder, a cord snaking from it to some sort of speaker sitting in the back of a truck parked on the other side of the garage. Lucas was basically a male version of his sister—tall and crazy skinny, with pasty skin and white-blond hair scooped up into some spiky anime-like 'do. Not usually my cup of soy chai latte, but I'm not gonna lie: a guy with a guitar? Pretty damn hot.

Behind Lucas, beneath shelves holding paint cans, and surrounded by drums and cymbals, sat the police deputy–slash–drum player. His short honey-blond hair was tousled and curly at the ends, his jaw shadowed with stubble darker than you'd expect a blond guy to have. His bare arms—shown off to great effect by an exceptionally clingy wifebeater—were tanned and so very, very defined.

Let me tell you, if I'd known how beautiful the deputy was, I'd have come to Lucas's rehearsals a lot sooner. The deputy's biceps were things of my late-night dreams. His pale blue eyes were too. And his broad shoulders. And his . . .

"Ready, Luke?" the deputy asked. Neither of them had noticed me.

"Yeah, I got it. Give me a four count."

The deputy nodded and banged his drumsticks together four times before pounding on the drums, while Lucas flicked at his guitar and began to sing. The walls rattled as the sound reverberated through the garage.

I wasn't in the mood for a concert and had things to do, so I took a step forward and gave two loud claps.

Lucas actually jumped. The deputy didn't react much except to smile over at me. He had perfect, movie-star teeth.

"Uh, can I help you?" Lucas asked.

Grinning, I sauntered deeper into the garage. "Don't recognize me?"

His cheeks flushed as I came close—very close. "Em-Emily?"

"Can't believe you didn't recognize me, dork," I said,

swatting at his arm. I looked over at the deputy and met his smile with one of my own. "Introduce me to your friend."

Lucas took a step back. "Megan's inside, Emily. We're gonna be canvassing clubs this week to advertise our gig on Saturday, and I want to make sure we don't suck before we do. So please—"

"Jared." The deputy stood up from behind his drums and extended a hand.

I went and took Jared's hand, shaking it and letting my fingers linger as he let go. His grip was strong.

"Ignore him," Jared said as he gave me a once-over. "He doesn't know how to behave when a pretty lady enters the room."

Rounding the drum set, I sat on the stool he'd just vacated. "A gentleman and a drummer, huh? So does this band only have the two of you?"

"You got it. We're the Bubonic Teutonics."

"So, what, you're like an albino White Stripes or something?"

Jared laughed, sending his Adam's apple bobbing up and down on his long neck. I could see small beads of sweat forming there, could smell something enticing in his perspiration. Some part of me wondered, *Is he the one?*

The one what? I wondered again, but only briefly. Somehow, as nighttime me, the unusual thought almost seemed to make sense.

"Yeah," he said. "Something like that. So, are you and Megan heading out somewhere?"

I needed to get closer to him to be sure. I decided to bat my eyes and tilt my head so that my hair brushed against my bare shoulders. From Jared's expression, it seemed to work.

"Totally," I said. "Wanna come? It'll be fun."

"I'm pretty sure I'm too old to be going places with sixteen-year-olds."

"You *are* too old," Lucas called. Having grown bored with the two of us, he'd gone to the truck and was fiddling with his guitar and the speakers. He strummed a cord, and a screeching sound echoed through the bare rafters above us.

Jared shrugged, the muscles on his broad, bare shoulders tensing tightly. "Sorry, guess you two are on your own. Just make sure it's a crowded place and you drive there. Can't be too careful after what happened to that poor girl last night."

"Ooh, you really are a deputy, aren't you?" I had to know if he was the one my brain was searching for. Leaning in slightly, I closed my eyes and inhaled.

I expected . . . I don't quite know what I expected. But he smelled off. He smelled *clean*, artificial, like the mix of man-made chemicals that are soap and shampoo. And though usually I thought that would be a good way to smell, a strange disappointment washed over me.

I didn't know how I knew, but he wasn't right. At least not the *right* this new version of me wanted. Still, he was so pretty to look at.

"Lucas, Mom told you to keep it down and—what the hell?"

The door leading into the house slammed shut, and I spun on the stool to see Megan standing there. She was dressed in her clothes from that morning, her long hair pulled back into a ponytail. She stiffened in surprise at the sight of me.

"Emily? Is that you?"

I raised my eyebrows. "Hey, what's up?"

"Hey, Meg," Jared said. "Your friend was just saying hi."

"Yes, she's distracting Jared and keeping me from practicing," Lucas said, still focused on tuning his guitar. "Get rid of her and then I'll keep it down."

Megan could only stare slack-jawed at me. "Emily?" she said again. "What are—Why are you dressed like that?"

"Come on, I look awesome," I said. Regretfully leaving Jared behind, I rounded the truck and grabbed Megan's arm. "I'm on a mission."

Speechless, Megan let me lead her back through the

door. I waved over my shoulder as I went inside. "Bye, Deputy."

He winked at me. "Nice meeting you. And remember to be safe."

"Always."

I shut the door and could hear the boys begin their song again. Shoving Megan, I said, "Why didn't you tell me that the deputy was basically a male model?"

Megan flinched away from me. "Is this some kind of joke? What are you talking about? That guy is twenty-one years old, Emily, and you were hanging on him like a frickin' groupie."

"How could I *not*?"

With a disgusted sigh, Megan stormed down the hall-way to her bedroom. I followed her in, went to the edge of her bed, and leaped on top of her messy comforter. I rested back on my arms and crossed my legs.

"I need you, Reedy," I said. "Been to Emily Cooke's blog today?"

Megan continued to gape. "What? No, I—," she started.

I waved my hand. "Didn't miss much, just a bunch of kids acting like they cared about the hot chick at school before she died. But you know Terrance? Down the street? He called me fat, so you and I are going to go to his house and verbally smack him down." I wagged my eyebrows.

"Maybe a little physical smackdown too."

Megan gawked at me.

"Hello?" I gestured toward her shoes in the corner. "Chop-chop, girl, put your shoes on. We've got things to do, teenage boys to humiliate—"

"Okay, stop!" Megan threw her hands in the air. "Back up, Em, 'cause you are flirting with my brother's friend, you're dressed like a giant slut, and you're acting like you've downed a cocktail of vodka and crack."

I rolled my eyes. "Oh, come on, we don't have time for this, just—"

Megan stormed forward and put her finger in my face. "No, listen, Em: You don't come barging into my house done up like this and get away without explaining yourself." She caught sight of my mud-splattered shoes and gaped at me. "How did you even get here, anyway? Did you walk all the way here by yourself? After what happened last night?"

Again I rolled my eyes, then looked away at Megan's walls. Her *art*. Scrawled paintings that showed no sense of depth or anatomy or, y'know, skill were tacked to the wall. Megan liked to pretend she was an artist, but I'd always known she was a straight-up poser. Instead of trying too hard to be one of the Cool Kids like in junior high, now Megan tried too hard to be one of the Mysterious Loners. She was always hiding herself, just like I did. Or used to do.

After tonight I was never going back to the old me.

Megan grabbed my arm and pulled me toward her door. "No, Emily, I don't know what's going on, but you're not yourself. Someone just got frickin' killed a few streets up from you last night, and now you're walking around dressed like *this*—"

I yanked my arm from Megan's grasp. "I feel fine," I said. "Better than fine. I feel *amazing*." I got in Megan's face and grabbed her shoulders. "Don't worry about me, Reedy. Focus on the goal: Terrance Sedgwick down the street?"

Megan sighed again. "Em, I am not—"

I shook her, and she scowled. "Just answer the question. Seriously, you know Terrance, right?"

"He's a fat jerk. What about him?"

"Let me show you."

I pushed her around her bed toward the laptop on her desk. Shoving her down in her chair, I opened the laptop, clicked her browser, and got on to Emily Cooke's blog. A few scrolls down the page and Terrizzle's message was smack-dab in front of us.

I pointed, and Megan read what he wrote. "What a jerk! You are in no way fat." She gestured at the screen. "Is that what this is about? What Terrance wrote? Overcompensation is unhealthy, Emily."

I put out my arms and spun, modeling my outfit,

knowing that every part of me looked amazing. "I'm work-ing this top, though, aren't I? This is to lure Terrance into a trap and mess with him. Luring other guys is just an added bonus."

Megan slouched in her chair. After a moment, she said, "If I don't go with you, you're going over there by yourself? You're really going to go wander over to some strange guy's house, dressed like that?"

I nodded. "Well, yeah. It's not like anything bad is gonna happen to me. If I can survive a drive-by drink throwing, I can survive anything."

"What on earth are you talking about?" Megan asked.

I put on my best innocent face. "Nothing," I said. "So, decision time. You coming?"

With another sigh, Megan pushed herself to her feet. "Fine, I'll go with you. But we're taking my car, not walking."

"Wicked."

"Whatever." Megan slipped on her shoes before snag-ging her keys from a hook on the wall, and we headed into the cool night. I spread my arms and twirled down the wet concrete walkway toward the street, where Megan's car sat waiting.

Megan didn't say anything, just stomped past me. She unlocked the passenger door, banging it with her fist so that it popped open with a metallic creak. I ducked inside as she got into the driver's seat. Punching the gas, she turned the key in the ignition and the car belched before sputtering and dying. Cursing, Megan turned the key again. This time the car coughed to life. Megan flicked on the pale headlights and pulled out into the road.

"Little Rusty's on his last leg," I said. I felt for the seat lever and then lowered the back so I could lie down. Propping my heels atop the dashboard, I watched Megan as she drove. She kept her eyes on the road, her brows drawn tight and her lips pursed. Orange light from the streetlamps briefly lit up her scowl as we passed beneath them.

I stretched and waved my hand in her face. "Hello, Reedy? I just called your car Little Rusty. You're supposed to get all pissy and tell me not to call it that."

Megan ignored me. She stomped on the brakes, hard, and I lurched forward. Before I could react she cranked the steering wheel to the left and headed down a side street.

Lowering my feet, I sat up and peered out the window. We were heading down Roosevelt Street—the exact opposite direction of where I wanted to go.

"Hold up, Megan, you're going the wrong way."

She ignored me and kept driving.

Tugging her arm, I said, "Hey, don't be lame, we're supposed to go to Terrance's!" When she didn't stop, I popped the back of the seat up. "Okay, if this is about your brother and the deputy, don't be a freak. I wasn't going to *do* anything with them. The deputy was just cute and I wanted to say hi."

Megan let out an exasperated sigh and glanced at me. The green dashboard lights gave her pupils an unearthly glow.

"Okay, ew. But no, this isn't about my brother or his friend." She yanked the wheel to the right and turned down another street. "Or maybe it is. It's about the clothes, pawing at older guys, wanting to go after Terrance, all of it." She flicked her hand up in annoyance. "It's about you even telling me, 'Don't be a freak'! You don't say things like that, Emily. Something is really wrong with you right now that you apparently can't see, so I'm taking you home so you can go to bed and wake up and be yourself again."

I opened my mouth to protest. Without even looking at me, Megan held up a finger in my face and said, "Don't argue."

Suddenly the car felt horribly cramped. It was a cage of rusted steel surrounding me, hemming me in and stinking of cracked pleather and exhaust and ancient nacho cheese crusted into the backseat carpet. It didn't help that the warden of this little prison was Megan at her snippiest. I glared at the side of her pasty, long, giant-nosed face, and I hated her. I wanted to lunge at her and throw her to the ground, tower above her and make her realize that I wasn't some mousy little girl she could boss around.

Instead, glaring out the window, I got an idea.

"That's cool," I said. "You're right. This isn't me." I wrapped my fingers around the ancient window crank and forced the old gears to turn, lowering the window. Cool air rushed through the widening crack, catching my hair.

"Whatever," Megan said. "Terrance is a jerk, but we'll get him back some other way. Once you're no longer tripping on glue fumes or whatever is going on here."

"Oh, totally." By now the window was completely open. I stuck my head out and parted my lips to suck in a breath of fresh air. I opened my mouth and let my tongue loll out.

And then, while Megan ignored me to glower out at the dark street, I swiftly unlatched my seat belt, reached out of the window, and grabbed onto the ancient bike rack bolted to the top of Little Rusty. I hefted myself outside so that my heels straddled the door, then slanted back as far as my arms would let me.

I clung to the bike rack as the car raced down the dark suburban street at thirty-five miles per hour. Parked cars and trees whizzed by me, and the wind felt like it was trying to toss me to the hard asphalt that zipped past beneath, but I had no fear. I was in control here. The night, the wind, the car—I was their master.

I tilted my head back and let out a loud, howling laugh.

Megan's panicked voice screeched out of the car. "Emily! What are you doing?"

She never sounded panicked. She was scared out of her mind, and I loved it.

The car swerved as Megan momentarily lost control. I rode it like a surfer riding a wave and whooped in excitement. We were rushing by the forested park not far from my house. The car started to slow, so I tensed my legs, waited for the right moment—and leaped.

The car came to a sudden stop, brakes squealing like the poor little pig whose house wasn't strong enough to keep the big bad wolf from blowing it down. The driver's-side door creaked open and Megan jumped out, running back down the street, her terrified expression painted red by the car's taillights. She screamed my name, "Emily! EMILY!"

Hanging from a tree branch fifteen feet off the ground, I laughed down at her.

"Scared you, didn't I?"

Megan slowly came back to stand beneath me on the dark, empty road. Her car grunted and grumbled behind her like an addled old man. She gawked up at me, trying to say something.

Gazing down at her from the branch like it was nothing, I started to say something—about how much of a bitch she was for lying to me, and that she got what she deserved—when a sensation washed over me. A feeling that something I couldn't see was hovering right in front of me, looking at me with eyes I couldn't see. Just like in the darkened back-yard I'd used as a shortcut.

And then, something inside me shifted. I very suddenly realized that I was freezing, that everything had gone blurry, and that I was hanging what felt like a million miles above the road after jumping out of a moving car.

And with that realization came fear, a dread that coated me, because absolutely nothing made sense.

"Oh . . . what?" I whispered.

My body was much too heavy to hold anymore and my fingers gave, the bark of the thick branch rubbing my palms raw as I screeched and fell. I landed half against Megan and half against the asphalt, the heel on my left boot snapping and sending me sprawling. Correction: the heel on *Dawn's* boot snapping. That wasn't good.

No, nothing was good. Everything I'd just done, every-thing I'd said and every action I'd made, came back to me in an overwhelming rush. Shivering, I pushed myself to my feet and peered over at Megan. Even in the bloodred light from the brake lights and with my vision as blurry as it always is without glasses, I could the see the mixture of anger and confusion and hurt on her face.

"I—I don't know what—" Wrapping my arms around my chest, I whispered, "I need to go home."

"Yeah," she said, putting her arm around me to support me as we hobbled back to her car. "Yeah, you really do."

6

EM CEE AND EM DUB

The rest of the night was more or less a blur—literally, because I didn't have my glasses. Megan drove me home and made a point of walking me to my front door. I managed to get past my dad at his computer—he only noticed me out of the corner of his eye and greeted me as "Dawn"—before crawling up the stairs, going into my room, and hiding under my covers.

The entire time, my skin prickled as though every hair on my body had stood on end and was trying to leap free, and my fingernails and my toenails throbbed with the echoing pain you get the day after slamming your finger in a door. A massive headache beat at my temples. Add all that sudden and reasonless pain to my stinging palms and it's a wonder I ever managed to fall asleep, but I did, like I'd just spent the day running a marathon and even the aching joints that came with that couldn't keep my exhausted body from unconsciousness.

I woke up the next morning before my alarm went off. For a few bleary, amazing moments, I lay there and thought, *What a weird dream.*

That was when my palms began to itch. I held them up and saw little bits of skin hanging free, and spots of dried blood scabbing over.

I kicked the covers off—I was still wearing the clothes I'd taken from Dawn's closet, sans boots. Fumbling for my glasses, I slipped them on my face—which felt sticky and cold with day-old makeup. Groaning, I flipped myself onto my stomach and pushed myself up. My pillow looked as wretched as I felt, streaked red and purple and black from the makeup I'd neglected to wash off the night before.

"Crap," I muttered.

Toppling out of bed, I caught sight of myself in the mirror. The gold shirt was wrinkled and lopsided, my hair was tangled and ratted, my face clownish. I caught sight of my boobs just sort of hanging there like a desperate D-list celebrity's version of cleavage. Immediately I hugged my chest to hide it.

Memories of sidling up to Lucas and Jared the night

before seeped into my sleep-addled brain. I had never let anyone see me so exposed, not since puberty brought the changes that made me lumpy and curvy, something to hide under baggy clothes. But all that work to go unnoticed went away last night—I'd gone out half-naked and flaunted all my flaws.

What did the fair-haired duo that were Bubonic Teutonics think? I remembered Jared's cocky smile. What if that smile wasn't him liking what he saw—what if he was laughing at me? And the way I'd talked to him! Good girls didn't act like that! *I* didn't act like that.

I turned away from the mirror, my stomach roiling. Was I sick? I once saw an episode of one of those hospital dramas where a girl got some spore in her brain and started coming on to one of the doctors, driven into insane lust by what amounted to a trivial bit of dust caught in her neurons. Had something like that happened?

Except—what about leaping out of my bedroom window? Bounding down a street after a car, jumping over fences? Climbing onto a frickin' *moving car*? How was it even possible for me, Emily Webb of all people, to do things like that without ending up a bloody splat on the concrete? I am the least graceful person I know. When I was seven and in dance class, I always played a tree or a bush or something in the recitals—stationary objects. And even then, half the time I managed to trip over my own feet while the parents in the audience tried not to laugh and the other little dancers glared at me for ruining their big night.

But that wasn't the worst thing. Even while I stood there, shaking and feeling like I was about to vomit all over my bedspread, part of me still liked the way I'd felt the night before.

Some guy on the street had been a jerk, and I'd gotten back at him. I saw a cute guy I wanted to talk to, and I talked to him (even though it was in a kind of slutty way), and the world didn't end. I leaped around like a video game character, like some sort of superhero, bounding over fences and racing down streets without breaking a sweat.

And all of it had felt so, so good. I'd felt confident for the first time in my life. Felt like I could do anything I wanted.

It was like, the older I got and the more I saw the other kids around me grow up, the more I harbored the fantasy of one day being a secret, perfect version of me. I'd always wished that I could be self-assured and pretty and super-athletic like the heroines I'd grown up idolizing: a Buffy, a Sydney Bristow, an Ellen Ripley.

But that wasn't supposed to become reality. It just didn't happen. None of this was possible. None of it.

It had all started the night Emily Cooke died. The same night she left her house and died was the same night all this began happening to me.

And then an idea popped into my head. A strange, totally crazy idea: What if the way I was behaving was how Emily Cooke *always* behaved? I didn't know much about her, other than that she was pretty and popular and had seemed confident in herself. Could it be that maybe Emily Cooke was . . . in me, somehow? Like maybe her angry spirit was planning to use me to avenge her murder?

I had felt, after all, like some new Emily had possessed me. And there had been those two times the night before when I'd quite clearly felt as though some unseen presence was hovering right in front of me, observing me.

Maybe it was a bit of a leap. But she did die only a few streets away. We did share the same name. And, come on, I was flipping around like I'd become the newest member of Cirque du Soleil—maybe spirits weren't so far outside the realm of possibility.

And if the presence I felt *wasn't* Emily C.'s spirit, then I didn't know what that meant. Only that the thought chilled me even more than thinking a ghost was controlling me like a puppeteer.

I sat on the edge of my bed, cradling little stuffed Ein in my lap, my eyes aimed at the floor for what felt like hours, all these conflicting emotions and thoughts swirling inside my head as I tried to understand what was going on and what I should do about it.

My clock's glowing numbers told me that it was 6:14. I was up an hour before usual. I couldn't stay here, trapped in my room, thinking about the weirdness of last night. I had to get out, do something normal.

I showered and got dressed in jeans and my baggiest hoodie before anyone else in the house was up. I shoved Dawn's wrinkled clothes and her broken boots into my closet—they were her clubbing clothes, so I hoped she wouldn't miss them right away—then tore the makeup-stained case off my pillow and tossed it into the laundry bin in the hallway. Just as my dad and stepmom's alarm went off and I heard Dawn rousing in her bedroom, I flung my backpack over my shoulder, left the house, and began the long walk to school.

"Where were you this morning?"

I hunched over my tray of steaming, overcooked sirloin steak–like substance, pushing around serrated carrots with my little plastic spork. Megan slammed her books on the lunch table beside me and sat down.

"Hey," I muttered, then shoved a bite of carrots into my mouth. I couldn't meet Megan's eyes, not after the way I'd acted, especially without knowing what had caused my massive mood swing so I could at least explain.

All around me the lunchroom hummed with noise. I looked up from my tray, away from Megan. Girls and guys sat at their tables, eating and laughing and chatting. Well, some of them, anyway. There were still tables of kids who seemed like they'd never smile again. A little memorial to Emily Cooke had been hastily put together on a corkboard near the cafeteria entrance, a picture of her stapled in the center and surrounded by poems and letters her friends had written. The cafeteria seemed emptier than usual. I guess some people had decided to stay home.

Fingers snapped in front of my face, and grudgingly I gave Megan my attention. Her brow was furrowed, her lips tight. I could hold her eyes for only a second before slumping back over.

"Seriously, Emily," she whispered. "You act all crazy last night, then you can barely speak and I have to take you home, and then you're not even there this morning when I come to pick you up. I didn't see you in Ms. Nguyen's class, and I thought something had happened, but I saw you in the hall. . . ."

I'd skipped homeroom. I didn't want to have to sit next to Megan, face what had happened. Lot of good that had done me.

I dropped my spork in the mush of food, swallowing the lump that had risen into my throat. "Sorry, I'm really sorry," I said. "I really don't know what happened. I had, like . . . a mood swing or something, I guess."

Megan let out a sharp laugh. "Mood swing? I've had mood swings, Em, but nothing like that. It's like your mood swung so hard it tossed you around the bar or something. I mean, you just about mounted the deputy in my garage last night."

I shoved my tray away. How I must have appeared last night to that stoner guy, let alone to Lucas and to Jared and to Megan . . .

I suddenly wasn't hungry.

"I think I might be . . . sick or something? I don't know. I didn't tell you, but . . . it happened before, sort of. The mood swing. Two nights ago. The night Emily Cooke died."

"The other Emily? You think . . ."

I shrugged and hunched down. "I don't know. I mean, they say that she acted strange and then just left her house all of a sudden, dressed in pajamas, right? The same night I dressed all differently and almost did the same thing. Maybe . . ." I hesitated, not sure if I should share my "possessed by Emily Cooke's angry ghost" theory. I decided against it and went with the more rational explanation. "I thought maybe there is something going around, like what happened to me is maybe what happened to Emily Cooke and that's why she died."

Megan let out a long breath. "So when you said you thought it could have been you yesterday . . ."

"Yeah," I said. "Maybe it really could have been."

Megan yanked me up by the arm before I could react. My seat squeaked backward and a few guys at a table nearby stopped talking to check us out. I remembered very suddenly Terrance Sedgwick's stupid message, and I wondered if those guys had seen it, what they were thinking now as they watched me make a scene. Though I longed to regain the self-confidence I'd had last night and not care what anyone thought of me, I just couldn't. Instead I blushed and gently shook Megan off.

"No, come on," she whispered to me. "We're going to the nurse, right now. If there's something wrong with you, we're going to fix it."

"Yeah, okay. Okay."

Leaving my tray behind, I picked my backpack up from the floor and followed Megan between the tables, catching bits of conversation as I did. I felt like everyone was watching me as I passed, somehow knowing what had happened the night before.

"Hey, watch it!"

Megan stopped suddenly, and I nearly knocked her over. There was a thud and a clatter as leather smacked against the linoleum and pens scattered across the floor.

I peeked up to see that Megan had dropped her backpack while almost walking into a guy I'd never seen before. An incredibly cute guy—tall, slender, with black hair and amazingly sharp eyebrows that gave him the whole broody bad-boy aura. He was even wearing black jeans and a black leather jacket, like he'd just stepped out of an old James Dean flick and was on his way to go race cars in trenches like the causeless rebel he was.

Megan scowled down at her dropped backpack. "Twice in one day, Patrick. You seriously need to watch where you're going."

The guy regarded Megan with those dark, wise-beyond-his-years eyes. Then he muttered, "Sorry." There was a hint of an accent in his voice, but what kind I couldn't tell.

He sat down at the nearest table and pulled a sack lunch from his backpack. With an annoyed sigh, Megan bent down to pick up her bag and the few pens that had fallen out. As she did, I caught a whiff of something intensely . . . manly. Musky and heavy, like cologne.

I remembered the night before, the whole smell thing. The odors around me had been intense—but not as intense as whatever this smell was. And unlike Deputy Jared's refreshing spring-clean scent, this one made my stomach flutter.

Is he the one?

The thought was distant, very distant, coming from

some hidden recess of my mind. But the pull to *sniff* was inescapable. I had to know.

Glancing around to make sure no one was watching, and trying not to flare my nostrils like a freak, I sniffed in the direction of the new guy—and that's when another guy popped up in front of me and shoved a piece of paper in my face.

"Hey, want to go to a party?"

"Uh . . ." Not knowing what else to do, I took the paper—it was hot pink and used about a dozen different fonts to basically say that there was, duh, a party. Classy. Holding the invitation by its corners, I scanned its Comic Sans and Papyrus font–scribed message, sure that I'd been handed this by mistake.

"Leave her alone, Spencer." Megan was beside me again, her dropped belongings all gathered.

The guy who'd handed me the paper—short, funny Spencer from homeroom—ducked his head. "Hey, sorry, Megan, I just thought you guys might want to come, and I wanted to invite you before you left lunch. Mikey Harris is throwing his usual beginning-of-the-year party, and it's also gonna be a tribute to Em Cee, you know? A way for us all to get together and remember her."

I pushed my glasses up my nose and met Spencer's eyes. "Em Cee?"

"Sorry, I mean Emily Cooke. I had a class a few years ago with you and her in it, and she was Emily C. and you were Emily W., so in my head I shortened your names to, uh . . ." He laughed shyly. "Em Cee and Em Dub."

I could feel my face go hot, and I really didn't know why. "Em Dub, huh?" I said.

"Wonderful, thanks for sharing, Spencer," Megan said. "We're not interested in any parties being thrown by Mikey Harris and his friends." Snatching the invitation from my hand, she slapped it on the table next to the new guy and put her face next to his. "Here you go, Patrick. Join their club. Then you can start bumping into me on purpose like those snottards do, instead of doing it because you're incapable of watching where you're going."

The new guy blinked, looked askance at the neon pink piece of paper, blinked once more, and resumed eating. Megan grabbed my arm and began to pull me toward the lunchroom door now that the path was clear. Once her back was to us, Spencer gave me another invitation.

"You never know," he whispered to me. He put his hand in the air as we walked away. "Okay. Well, bye!"

"Bye," I said quietly. I glanced again at the invitation. Emily Cooke's name jumped out at me—maybe because it was in a huge font, bolded, and italicized. Or maybe it was just because I had her on the brain. And though last night I'd been wondering who I myself had become, as I read Emily Cooke's name just then I thought, *Who were you?*

"Throw that away," Megan demanded as she dragged me through a cluster of kids.

I crumpled the pink invitation, but when Megan's back was to me, I shoved it into my pocket.

As I did, my eyes drifted back to the new guy sitting at his table, alone, seemingly unfazed by his run-in with Megan's massive hostility while he bit into a pear. He observed the view out the big bay windows that lined the back of the lunch hall, apparently engrossed by the blue peaks of Mount Rainier on the clear horizon. The farther we got from him, the fainter the musky cologne I smelled became, until I couldn't smell anything but rehydrated mashed potato product and greasy gravy from the cafeteria kitchens.

I turned back to Megan. "That guy," I said. "You ran into him earlier?"

Megan snorted. "Yeah, he's some new guy, Patrick something. He almost knocked me over in second period too."

We brushed past a few teachers standing in the mostly empty hall. When they were out of earshot, I asked, "Does he always smell like that?"

Megan guided me around a row of lockers toward the

front offices. "Uh, smell like what?"

"I dunno. He was wearing some sort of cologne. He smelled . . ." Perfect. Amazing. Stimulating. "Nice," I finished.

"First the deputy, now the new guy?" Megan groaned. "What the frick, Emily, are you suddenly going all boy crazy? Are you seriously transforming into one of the bobble-headed idiot chicks we go to school with?"

"What?" I said. "No, I . . ." I trailed off. "No, I'm not."

"Let's just get you to the nurse." Eyes filled with anger, she muttered, "Trust me, Emily. You'd be better off dead like the other Emily than turning 'normal' like one of *them*."

"That's a bit harsh."

"No," Megan said, "it's not."

I didn't want to argue. When Megan got riled up, talking to her was impossible. So I kept silent, and I wondered, would it really be so bad to be the Emily Webb I'd been last night full-time? My body hadn't seemed so clumsy and bloated. I had felt like I didn't have any cares at all. Sure, I'd acted brazen to complete strangers, performed a few dangerous feats that could have left me dead. What if I could learn to get that under control?

But what if I couldn't?

After a long moment I said, "Yeah. Let's get me fixed up."

SOUNDS LIKE A PLAN

"Well, as far as I can tell, girls, you're both completely healthy." The school nurse, Mrs. Hawkins, stood in front of me and smiled. Her blond perm glowed under the bright fluorescents, making her seem like a grown-up and wrinkled version of one of those chubby angels you see hanging in church-lady bathrooms.

I studied the walls, not sure what to say. I mean, I felt fine *now*, but I knew I couldn't seriously be *healthy*. Across from where I sat atop her little examining table there were all sorts of posters tacked to the walls. One about the food pyramid, another about proper brushing, one with tiny writing all about the dangers of sex. They were all faded, the laminate peeling from their edges. I wondered what the school board had deemed healthy to put on a poster about sex back in 1986 when these posters were plastered here.

"She's *not* okay, Mrs. Hawkins," Megan insisted. She stood much too close to the nurse, towering over the short woman. "She was dressing all trashy, coming on to my brother's twenty-one-year-old friend, sneaking out of her house. There was even something about drive-bys with drinking." She waved her hand at me. "I mean, come on! Slutty is *not* Emily!"

Mrs. Hawkins rested a pudgy hand on Megan's arm. A little gold chain she had round her wrist slid beneath the sleeve of her Lane Bryant blazer.

"No offense, dear, but you two are teenagers," she said. "In my experience, if it's not drugs or alcohol driving you kids crazy, it's hormones. Girls develop at different rates, and perhaps Emily is just . . . developing."

Megan let out an exasperated sigh and stomped away. "Please! Emily *developed* when we were eleven."

Self-consciously, I wrapped my arms around my chest as Mrs. Hawkins inspected me. I had felt more aware of my stupid chest the past couple days than I had in years, and I didn't like that at all. Being in fifth grade with everyone else still flat as a board, and me . . . It was just easier to cover things up, keep quiet, and hope everyone would forget I was different.

Megan turned back to face Mrs. Hawkins. "She never acted like this back then, and even if she was going to now, why just for a couple hours a night? And on the same night as Emily Cooke lost her mind, went walking in the dark in a nightie or whatever, and got herself killed? Is that something that 'developing' girls do?"

Raising her fist to her pursed red lips, Mrs. Hawkins let out a prim little cough. "Well, yes, you have a point," she said after a moment. Leaning in toward Megan and me, she lowered her voice. "Honestly, girls, there's only so much I can do as a school nurse. I'm only here because I taught Health and Sex Education last year, and I was going to be let go this year unless I took this post."

Reassuring.

Shuffling away, she went to a file cabinet near the door and yanked it open. She said, "Emily, you seem fine from what I can tell, but if you're really concerned you should have your mother take you to a see a real doctor."

Nonchalantly, Megan said, "Her mother's dead."

Mrs. Hawkins spun around from the filing cabinet, one hand fluttering to her chest. In her other hand she clenched a bunch of pamphlets. "I'm so sorry, dear. I didn't know."

"Oh, it's all right, it happened when I was two," I said.

"Still, dear," Mrs. Hawkins went on. "The relationship between a girl and her mother is an important one. I can't imagine what it would be like to not have had my mother show me the ropes growing up."

If I wasn't uncomfortable before, well, I surely was then. The last thing I wanted to talk about with the school nurse was growing up mommy-less. And so I just said, "I have my father and my stepmother. One of them could take me, I guess."

Her plump cheeks rising into a smile, Mrs. Hawkins handed me the pamphlets. "Well, I'm glad to hear that. Now take a look at these and see which one you feel fits your problem. I was a girl once myself, and I know all about the moods we get, but if you think it's more . . ."

I held the pamphlets side by side. The first one read, "From Bliss to Blah: The Blight of Bipolarism." The next said, "So You're Going to Be an Unwed Teenage Mother?"

"Thank you." Grabbing my backpack from the table beside me, I leaped down to the floor. I felt unnerved—Megan had been more than a little forthcoming about what had happened last night, though thankfully she'd left out the part about my jumping out of her car—and I couldn't help but think Mrs. Hawkins was thinking how much of a freak I was.

Before the nurse could say anything else, I yanked open the door and stepped outside. The nurse's office was connected to the front office lobby, and old secretaries milled about, deep in discussion—about how to keep teenagers from rioting or how to handle uppity parents or whatever.

I marched out of the office and into the hall. Lunch was long over and fourth period had started. I realized I should have gotten a note from Mrs. Hawkins, but I decided I'd much rather get yelled at by my English teacher than go get poked and prodded by the nurse again.

"Hey, Em, wait up!"

Megan ran up to me in the hallway and took my arm. "Well, that was a waste," she grumbled. "Remind me never to get seriously injured at school with her as our potential lifesaver."

I glanced down at the pamphlets, then unzipped my backpack and shoved them inside. I wondered if there was a pamphlet on how to handle sudden-onset adolescent ghost possession. That could have been actually informative.

"So, we need a plan," Megan said as we walked. "Because you probably won't be able to see a doctor tonight, so I should come over and keep watch, make sure you don't do anything stupid."

I stopped and looked at Megan, part of me suddenly not wanting her to be there later. It was that secret, hidden part of me again, the one that daydreamed about being some sort of comic-book hero.

Flipping her head, she sent her long hair cascading down

her back. "What's that look for?" she sniped.

I hadn't realized I was giving her a look, so I twisted my head away. "Sorry, it's just . . . Maybe it won't happen again. I feel fine now, anyway."

"Don't be dumb," Megan said. "Earlier you were worried you were going to get yourself killed because you couldn't control yourself when you had those mood swings or whatever."

I didn't say anything. The change that had happened the night before was freaktastic, yes, but . . . what if I let it happen again? What if I didn't have Megan there, watching over me as I turned from dowdy lady into super-tramp? I could feel those sensations, experience that addictive, liquid grace. . . .

Get into more trouble that I'd have to face when I woke up the next morning, normal once more.

She shook me. "Hello?" she said. "So we have a plan then?"

"Yeah," I said. "Sounds like a plan."

"Hey there, Leelee, how was school?"

I dropped my backpack by the front door as it slammed shut behind me, and forced myself to give my dad a smile. There was a loading screen on his monitor, so he actually bothered to swivel around in his chair to greet me, his bifocals crooked and a headset clinging atop his balding head. He waved me over for a hug.

"It was fine."

I bent and hugged him, burying my head in his neck. He smelled so very dad-ish, like Old Spice and a little bit of sweat and a whole lot of reassurance. I clung to him a little too long, I guess, because he whispered in my ear, "Hey, kid, something wrong?"

I let him go and forced another smile. What was I supposed to tell him? *Yes, Dad, there's a whole lot of wrong going on, because the last two nights I seem to have developed a split personality that made me leap around like I had my own ninja wire stunt team, which—honestly?—felt completely awesome and exhilarating, but which still freaked me out in the morning. And now Megan thinks I'm sick, and I'm afraid the angry spirit of a dead classmate has taken me over, and the school nurse seems to think I'm either pregnant or mentally unstable. Care to run me to the hospital—or the local psychic—to see if any of those are the case?*

"No, nothing's wrong, just had a long day." He continued to look at me quizzically, not quite sure if I was telling the truth, so I asked, "And how was *your* day?"

His face lit up. "Oh, busy, busy. The guild had a raid earlier and we totally kicked butt, but I completely ran out of potions and needed to hit the auction house."

"Oh. Sounds . . . neat." I started to turn toward the stairs, then bit my lip and turned back. "Mind if I watch a little?"

"Yeah! Grab a seat."

Our front door opens up into the dining room and the little foyer where my dad has his computer, so I dragged over one of the dining chairs and scooted in close. Patting me on my back, Dad turned back to his game and started pressing keys to highlight monsters and kill them.

I sat there for a while, watching him play, not really understanding what exactly he was doing but not really wanting to go up to my room and be by myself, either.

It had been ages since I'd hung out with my dad. I mean, we used to, a lot. For a long time it was just me and him— Dad and his little Leelee staying up late watching TV, going out to movies every weekend, reading Alan Moore comics to each other as bedtime stories. He religiously took me to practice when little me was sure that dance was my calling in life, never missing a recital no matter how crappy my part or how late he had to work at whatever construction job he may have had that week. When I dropped out of that, he let me take tae kwon do classes until I realized that I wasn't meant to be an action hero either. He seemed relieved when all I asked for on my next birthday was a new bookcase and a bunch of DVDs of old horror movies.

But I got older, and he got older. He met my stepmom, and she and Dawn moved in. I started having more homework and ended up spending most of my free time with Megan or up alone in my room—I mean, I'd started to, y'know, *develop*—and though he was my dad, there were a lot of things that were easier to talk to Megan about. Not that it much mattered, since my stepmom took my place for evening TV, and when Dad didn't have a construction job to go to, he now had his game to occupy his time.

So it was nice to just sit there with him, the two of us alone at home sharing in the fun of pixels fighting other pixels on a screen with glowy effects swirling around.

I thought again about everything as I watched him jab at his keyboard, eyes darting back and forth as he moved his character around. I wanted so, so bad right then to be just me and him again, back before junior high and high school, back before Megan and Dawn and my stepmom. . . . Maybe then I could have asked for his help.

Instead I coughed. When that failed to get his attention, I jabbed at his shoulder.

"Hmm?" He darted a glance at me briefly before focusing once again on his monitor.

"Yeah, so, Megan wanted to come over tonight. Is that okay?"

"No!" Smashing his index finger over and over on the number one key at the top of his keyboard, he muttered a swear under his breath. I saw his character fall down dead on-screen and everything go gray as he turned into a little animated ghost.

"I hate gnomes." He lowered his headset and turned to me. "What was that? Something about Megan?"

"Yeah," I said. "Can she come over, maybe stay the night?"

Before, he would have asked me why, or maybe even offered to make a night of it for us, conveniently forgetting that we likely had homework so that we could stay up late having a *Nightmare on Elm Street* marathon.

"Oh, sure thing," he said. "You two have fun." With that, he returned to his game and started running his character's ghost back to its body.

And that was the end of father-daughter time.

Returning my chair to its place under the dining room table, I picked up my bag and went upstairs to my room. Then I sat at my computer, opened up the browser to Google, and typed in "Emily Cooke."

I scrolled through the search results, ignoring the links I'd already clicked on. I muttered to myself, "So, other Emily: Who were you?"

I found a few things I hadn't the day before, distracted

as I'd been by Terrance Sedgwick's post about me on Emily Cooke's blog. But following a series of links revealed that Emily Cooke didn't just have a blog—she had her own web page. Nothing super fancy, probably made with one of those programs from a box, but it was classier than most high schooler web pages I'd seen.

The site was full of poetry and sketches and whimsical watercolor paintings. There was a gallery of black-and-white photographs that I weren't sure were ones she just liked, or ones she'd taken herself. Either way, I found them striking—photos in profile of people I didn't recognize, of interesting objects in a home, all in sharp contrast that seemed to reveal some flaw that made them so imperfect that they became . . . perfect.

None of the stories or poems I read seemed to reveal any latent superpowers—though I guess if Emily Cooke was really the long lost daughter of the Incredibles family, she wouldn't broadcast it on the internet. Mostly, her writing revealed that she had a pretty sly sense of humor. One story, a thinly veiled tale about an alien conspiracy nut going all Chicken Little that just had to be about Ms. Nguyen, left me in a giggling fit that, for a few moments, made me forget all about the craziness of the past few days.

I wasn't getting anything from this little excursion into Emily Cooke's virtual world that screamed, *Girl superhero*

that is puppet-mastering you from beyond the grave!
Mostly, I just realized that maybe there had been more to
Emily Cooke than I'd thought.

And now she was gone. All that was left of her was text
and pictures on a computer screen.

"Is it you?" I whispered as I studied a self-portrait of
Emily Cooke. "Are you doing this?"

Her eyes were pale in the black-and-white photo, and
she was half smiling, like she did know all the answers but
couldn't tell me. And as I studied her face—her slender
nose, her arched brow, her stylishly cut blond hair—I felt
a strange connection. Maybe it was just that she seemed
to like words and interesting images the same way I did.
Maybe it *was* that her spirit was still around, hovering over
me for some reason I couldn't know.

Maybe it was something else altogether.

I stared at the screen for a long time. Then I closed
the browser and got ready to sit around and wait for the
change—the possession, the sickness, whatever it was—to
come and make me into a whole new girl.

The red LED display on my alarm clock read 7:55 p.m.

After delving into the online world of Emily Cooke, I'd
set about completing my homework and finished by six. I ate
a quick dinner downstairs and was done by six thirty—or

almost, anyway. I could barely get down half a sandwich, my stomach felt so tight with nervousness. I tried reading, browsing online, watching a DVD, but it was useless— I couldn't concentrate. Yesterday and the day before, my "mood swing" had come at a little after eight o'clock, when it was fully dark outside. That time was rapidly approaching, and there was no sign of Megan.

I was torn. I still longed to let go and become the Emily Webb of the night before. But I was also still unsure about the whole thing, deeply afraid of what this could all mean. The more nervous and conflicted I became, the more I knew: Megan needed to be here. Change or no change, she was the one and only person I could rely on.

I had called Megan five times between seven o'clock and 7:55. She hadn't answered once. Back against my headboard, legs spread out over my bedspread and Ein cradled firmly in lap, I stared straight ahead at nothing, waiting.

I peeked over at my clock. 7:59.

Taking a breath, I reached over to the cell where it rested atop my desk, flipped it open, and scrolled down to select "Reedy." The phone rang . . . and rang . . . and rang.

"You have reached the voice mailbox of . . . 'Megan Reed.' Press one to leave a—"

I snapped shut my cell and tossed it back on my desk. "This was your plan, Megan," I muttered. "Where are you?"

The clock ticked over to eight o'clock.

8:01. 8:02. 8:03.

A sudden clattering and buzzing from my desk made me jump. The cell phone was vibrating where I'd tossed it, the display screen lit up: 8:04.

Clutching Ein, I grabbed the cell, opened it, and put it to my ear. Before I could even say anything, I heard Megan on the other end.

"Sorry, Em, I'm sorry I'm not there. I tried to get away, but my mom is making us have some stupid family night."

"What?" I said. Dread billowed into my stomach. "Megan, you're supposed to be here, you said it was a plan."

"I said I'm sorry," she snapped. Her voice was crackly, and I could hear muffled traffic in the background. "My mom found out about Emily Cooke this morning, and she's been freaking out like it was me or Lucas who died. She made us all go to dinner, and now I have to drive home and play Parcheesi or something with her."

Gripping Ein even tighter, I flopped over onto my side, away from the clock. "I really need you here. Please, Megan . . ."

"I can't, Emily. I'm really sorry. You told your dad about this, right? Maybe ask him to watch you. Or chain yourself to the bed or something—just don't leave the house, okay?"

I thought about my dad, who was probably downstairs

with my stepmom, watching reruns.

"Emily? You still there?"

"Yeah," I said, "I'm still here."

Megan sighed. "I'm almost home, so I need to hang up. Just please, please, please don't do anything stupid, okay? Promise me."

"I promise," I said.

"Okay." Megan sounded unsure. Another item on the rapidly increasing list of Ways Megan Never Sounded Before the Other Day. "Call me if you start to feel weird or anything, all right? I'll drop everything and come over there, no matter how much my mom complains. Talk to you later."

Before I could say good-bye, the phone clicked dead.

I sat there for a long moment, the phone still to my ear. I knew I should do something to prepare, just in case. Megan was right, maybe I needed to chain myself to my bed or something. I'd done some dangerous stuff without even thinking twice. I might do worse. I might get hurt.

Slowly I rolled over and peered at the clock.

8:11. 8:12. 8:13.

I held my breath, waiting. It had happened yesterday at 8:14. The cramps, or the seizure, whatever it was.

"So," I said aloud as I watched the clock, "it's just you and me now, other Emily. Uh, if it is you. It's probably not, is it?"

The clock still read 8:13.

I clenched my fists. "This is stupid. Of course this isn't you. Ghosts aren't real."

I squinted, making the clock's number blur before opening my eyes wide again. As before: 8:13.

"But just in case, if it is you? Try not to get me killed."

The room remained silent. Nothing rattled in response to my talking. No ghostly moans, no slamming doors. And then, finally, the clock changed. 8:14.

Nothing happened.

8:15. 8:16.

Still nothing.

I let out the breath I'd been holding, my body relaxing. It wasn't going to happen. I wasn't going to change.

"Not tonight, huh, other Emily?" I muttered.

I thought I'd be relieved. It was over. It wasn't going to happen.

But I wanted it too. I wanted to be her. I wanted to just escape the dreary, mundane life I'd buried myself in, even if it was only for one more night.

"No," I muttered. Holding up Ein so that we were nose to snout, I said, "I can't think like this. I can't want to be like—"

I gasped as the pain tore through my gut. Retching, I grabbed my stomach and curled into a ball on my bed, grinding my teeth and clenching my eyes closed as nausea swirled inside of me, that same poisonous, vomitous feeling I'd had the night before.

"Oh God," I wheezed. "Oh God . . ."

Then it was over. Much quicker than before.

And as I lay there, surveying my surroundings through glasses that now made my room a blurry mess of beige and black, I said to myself, "Actually, *yes* to escaping a dreary, mundane life."

Sitting up, I reached my arms over my head, stretching. My body felt rigid, tight, like I hadn't used it correctly in hours. Since last night, at least. I stretched out my legs, kicking Ein to the floor, where he tumbled belly up in the corner.

As I moved my legs, my pocket crinkled. I reached in and pulled out a crumpled wad of pink paper. Smoothing it open, I took off my glasses so I could read the hideous mishmash of fonts on the invitation Spencer had pressed into my hand earlier that day.

The show must go on, I read. *Mikey's Third Annual Start of School Bash is what you need to raise your spirits. Come remember and celebrate the life of our friend Emily Cooke with others who knew and miss her.*

Urges flashed in my head, the same ones as the night before: *Dominate. Find the one with the* right *scent. Prepare.* I needed to do these things.

My daytime self had spent so much time, so many *years*, wasting away in her quiet little shell. A party seemed a perfect place to reach for the limits. Someplace I could take my new self and . . . experiment.

I scanned the page. The party started at eight and was going on till eleven. Plenty of time for me to be fashionably late.

"Celebrate life?" I said to myself. "Sounds like a plan."

THANKS FOR THE PSA

"Stop whatever boring thing you're doing. We're going to a party."

Dawn sat at her desk, fingers poised above her laptop, as I burst into her room.

"Civilized people knock, Emily," she said. Clicking a few buttons on her computer, she saved whatever she was doing and turned in her chair to face me.

I strode to her desk and slapped the wrinkled pink invitation on top of it. "Read that," I said, "and tell me you don't feel like going to liven it up."

Dawn did just that, pushing a loose strand of her perfectly glossy hair behind her ear. She gave the page a withering look as she read.

"Uh, a high school 'bash'?" she said. "Not really my scene. And who says 'bash,' seriously?"

I laughed. "Pretentious high school kids who need our awesome selves around to show them how to have a good time. You in?"

Arching one of her perfectly plucked eyebrows, she turned her withering glance in my direction. "Dude, are you feeling all right?"

I pushed myself away from Dawn's desk and opened her closet. Digging through her clothes, I said, "I feel great! You said it yourself the other day, I'm finally unleashing the daring side you always knew I had." Taking out a pink top on its hanger, I held it up to myself and scrutinized its effectiveness in the mirror on Dawn's closet door. "I've been a boring, timid little girl for too long. It's time the world knows my name, have Webster's put my picture next to the definition of 'awesome.'"

I turned to her and shook the blouse. "What do you think?" I asked.

Hands pressed together in front of her face as though in prayer, Dawn could hardly hide her smile. She got to her feet and yanked the blouse from my hands.

"Pink is so not your color." Holding it up to herself, she said, "But my skin is, like, the perfect shade of tan to pull this off right now."

"So you're going to come with me?"

She laughed. "Oh, sure, dude. Screw my essay. High school party or no, I am so not missing out on your big public debut. I've put far too much work into you!"

Dawn quickly went all extreme makeover on me, holding up shirts and skirts and shoes. Frowning as she dug through her closet, she muttered about not being able to find these awesome thigh-high stiletto boots she loved. I pursed my lips and said nothing.

We found me a green tank that showed just enough cleavage. "But not too much," Dawn said. "You don't want to look gross and trashy like you did the other night—sorry, but it's true." We got changed and put on our makeup and were ready to go by nine. Giving my dad and her mom some excuse about going to see a movie, soon we were in Dawn's car and on our way.

Mikey Harris's house was one of those tall, stately McMansions you usually only see on those MTV faux-reality shows. The long driveway and most of the street in front of his endless lawn were filled with cars: half, the junky eight-hundred-dollar cars most teens get saddled with; the other half shiny sports cars that probably cost more than my dad makes in a year, gifts to the rich kids from their parents. The whole front of the house was lit up, and I could see shadows behind the bay windows. Some guys were hanging out on the porch sipping from red plastic cups.

I leaped from the car before Dawn even had it in park and headed up the front walkway, Dawn shouting at me to wait up while she got out of the car.

I sighed and halted for just a moment. As I waited, someone brushed a hand against my arm.

Recoiling, I turned to face whoever had touched me. It was a boy—or a man, I couldn't quite tell—wearing a tan Dick Tracy duster and a brimmed hat that hid his face in shadow.

"Can I help you?" I asked.

The guy cleared his throat. In a gravelly voice, he said, "Emily Webb? Daughter of—"

Dawn appeared then and grabbed me by the arm. "No thanks, not interested," she said to him as she pulled me up the driveway. "You know that guy?" she asked when he was out of earshot.

I looked back to see him still standing near the street, watching me, his face not visible.

"No," I said as I pulled my arm free of her grasp. "No clue. Just some drunk kid, I guess."

But he knew your name, some part of me shouted in my brain. *He asked whose daughter you were. That's* strange!

I ignored the voice. I didn't want to spend time worrying about some random drunk when there was fun to be had.

Leaving the weirdo behind us, we reached the guys sitting sentry outside the front door. They ogled us, eyes gleaming.

"Hey," I said. "Where's everyone? I expected more people."

One of the guys, a tall, gangly kid with no chin, smiled goofily. "They're all in the den watching some movie. You haven't missed much."

"A movie?" Dawn said, disappointed.

"Awesome," I said, striding past the guys to the front door.

As I reached for doorknob, the gangly guy's friend—squat and round with a shaved head—reached out a hand and brushed my thigh. I swatted him away.

"Hey," Dawn said, grabbing his wrist. "Don't—"

The guy held up both hands like he was facing off with police. "I just wanted to ask you if you wanted to hang with me inside. You know, get some alone time."

I said, "You couldn't handle me alone. Keep your hands to yourself, Short Round."

The gangly kid let out a low "Ooooh," and Dawn laughed. Then I was opening the front door and stepping into the house's massive foyer. Dawn whispered in my ear as we passed some kids hanging out on the stairs leading to the second floor, "You handled that like a pro, Em. I don't know what's come over you, but I like it."

"Get used to it," I said to her. "No more nice, boring Emily Webb."

Off the foyer, a pair of double doors opened onto a massive entertainment room. All the shiny, popular teenagers I saw every day at school were huddled together in pairs on the long couches and plush chairs set around the room. Everyone was silent, their eyes on the fifty-six-inch plasma hanging on the wall. The only sound came from the surround-sound speakers. The video was a home movie of a pretty blond girl dancing like a fool, hanging out around school, and cheering on friends at games.

Emily Cooke.

They were watching a movie about tall, pretty, popular, and extremely dead Emily Cooke while through the speakers some whiny chick playing a piano wailed a complete downer of a song. I saw some girls resting their heads against one another, sniffling back tears. A tall, well-built guy with slicked-over brown hair I recognized as our host, Mikey Harris, sat on the long black coffee table in front of the screen, deadly serious as he watched the movie play.

A bunch of puffy-eyed kids crying over the poor dead girl—not exactly how I expected my first high school party to be, let alone Mikey's "famous" start-of-school-year bash. This was, in a word, lame. No, "lame" doesn't even do this party justice. Let's break out some modifiers: completely lame. Massively lame. Humongously, utterly, humorlessly LAME.

Dawn and I stood behind everyone under the arch of the open double doors. Dawn muttered, "What is this, some sort of wake?"

I let out an irritated sigh, then took hold of Dawn's arm and led her back into the foyer. The people back here were sitting on the steps or in the chairs near the front door, drinking from plastic cups and talking quietly among themselves.

"Please tell me this isn't the type of party you always raved about," I hissed.

"Hey, don't look at me," she said. "I must have missed the part on the flyer where it said to dress in black and put on a mourning veil." Realization in her eyes, her mouth dropped open. "Wait a sec, they said this was a celebration of someone named Emily Cooke. Was that the girl who died?"

"Yeah. Even dead, the other Emily overshadows me."

Dawn let out a disgruntled sigh. "Well, you could have given me a heads-up, Emily. We're not exactly dressed appropriately." She gazed through the doorway at the kids, then turned away in thought. After a moment, she put her arm around my shoulder to guide me down the hall away from the milling teens. "Well, I guess maybe it's a good thing it's not so crazy here. It's your first party, it's probably good to start slow, maybe talk with some of the others about what happened to your friend. Besides, it's a school night. Your dad would kill me if I let you get too wild."

I grunted. I did not want slow. I wanted to blow these people's minds, for them to worship at my stylish yet affordable boots, for them to say, "Who's the cool new girl?" then gawk once they heard it was that quiet girl they never paid any attention to.

But before I could say anything, someone behind us called out, "Dawn? Dawn Michaels?"

We turned to see two perfectly pretty, perfectly bland girls by the stairs. I didn't recognize them, so I figured they were seniors.

"Oh my God, Emma!" Dawn squealed. "Lindsey!"

The two girls squealed right back and rushed over to pull Dawn into a bouncy, high-pitched hug.

"Oh, Dawn, we've missed you!" said the leggy one with the slick blond hair.

"I'm so glad to see you haven't forgotten us little people," said the one with the neck and the slick brown hair.

Both of them had big anime eyes surrounded by dark liner and giant white teeth. They reminded me of cartoon horses.

"No, of course not!" Dawn said.

"Are you here about Emily?" the blond one said. "It's so sad, isn't it? She was, like, only a year younger than us."

"And she was so pretty," the other one piped up.

"Actually, I was just bringing my sister to her first high school party." Dawn put her arm around my shoulder and pulled me over. "This is Emily—another Emily. You guys probably know her from around school."

The two girls looked me over, their faces falling slightly though they did their best to keep their perky smiles plastered on their overly bronzed faces. "No, can't say we do," Blondie Legs said.

"Hello," Necky Brunette said.

I scrunched my cheeks into a smile I so wasn't feeling, but said nothing. I was about to beg off and flee this dead party, take Dawn to find something more fun to do, when I heard noises coming from a room down the hall. Heavy thumps and some frat-boy-in-training trademark whoops.

Sounded like a place I could have some fun.

"Oh, you have to come tell us all about college," Blondie said, grabbing Dawn's hands.

Dawn bit her lip and looked between me and the two senior girls. "Do you mind, Em? I don't want you to feel like I'm ditching you, but there's nothing much going on, party-wise. . . ."

I waved my hand. "Nah, it's cool, go chat. I'll . . . mingle.

Uh, talk about my friend, reminisce, and all that."

Shrugging apologetically, Dawn let herself be pulled up the stairs.

The whoops from down the hall were joined now by loud, deep laughter. Following the sounds, I left behind the slow memorial music wafting from the main room and found myself at the entrance to Mikey Harris's giant kitchen.

Half a dozen guys stood around the island in the center of the kitchen surrounded by stacks and stacks of twelve-packs. One was ripped open and sat on the counter beneath the dangling pots and pans. Crushed, empty cans littered the countertop, some scattered across the black-and-white tiled floor.

I recognized several guys from the football team. The tallest and by far the hottest was Dalton McKinney, the star quarterback and one of the many princes of the Carver High campus. Clean-cut good looks, slender yet muscular build, close-cropped red hair, friendly green eyes, boyish freckles—he was the face of good ol' boy football and the unofficial leader of the team. I'd had a few classes with him, and he just seemed sickeningly nice, especially for a jock. He was always offering to help teachers after class and was tire-lessly kind toward nerds and jocks alike. He probably even assisted old ladies across the street and spent his weekends volunteering at the hospital as a candy striper.

I'd more or less written him off as practically perfect and intensely dull. So I felt a thrill seeing him here with his letterman jacket half hanging off, his hair a tousled mess, and letting out the loudest whoops of the gathered guys while he banged back two beers in quick succession.

With a satisfied gasp, he slammed the can down against the counter, crushing it with the top of his hand. The other guys cheered.

I leaned against the doorjamb and applauded.

With glazed eyes, all the guys turned in my direction. Their expressions immediately took on lecherous little twinkles. Deep down, I felt my daytime side's brief rush of embarrassment and then a surge of elation. She'd never before felt what it was like to be looked at like this.

Which is why I was around.

I strode into the room. "Looks like the real party's in here," I said. Reaching the island, I leaped to sit atop it, my butt hitting a pile of crushed cans and sending them clattering to the floor. "Mind if I join?"

One of the football players, a short, barrel-chested guy I recognized as Zach Nickerson, bent over the counter so that his head hovered above my lap, his eyes locked on mine.

"Baby, I've been waiting for you to join us all my life," he said. "What's your name? You new around here?"

103

I tilted my head back and laughed. "Are you kidding? I've gone to school with you since fifth grade. It's Emily."

Zach jerked back, scowling. "Not cool," he said. "Emily is—"

"Not Emily Cooke, doofus. Emily Webb. This is what I look like without the glasses. Take 'em off, I look hot. It's like magic."

Zach didn't seem to pay attention. Moments before he'd been whooping it up, but now he seemed immediately sobered. Muttering, "Not cool," under his breath once more, he grabbed the last can of beer from the twelve-pack on the counter and headed out into the hallway, one of the other guys following behind.

I jerked my thumb at Zach's retreating back and asked, "What's his problem?"

Dalton burst into a deep laugh. "He's drunk. Doesn't know how to handle someone out of his league like your fine self."

I wrinkled my nose at the stink of beer on his breath. But then I smelled something else. The musky, masculine, completely alluring cologne I'd caught scent of earlier in the cafeteria, coming from the new guy.

No—it wasn't the same smell, not exactly. It was close enough to make a weirdly awesome tingling sensation happen in my stomach, but it was different enough that I knew it wasn't what I'd smelled earlier. It felt off—enough so that the still mysterious, unknown part of my brain whispered, *Not the one* even as it also whispered, *Keep him close.*

And there was another smell. Something flowery and gross. That was when I remembered: Dalton McKinney, football star, was dating Nikki Tate, head cheerleader. A match made in high school cliché heaven.

Dalton hefted up a stack of twelve-packs and set them on the counter in front of me. He ripped the cardboard open, grabbed a beer for himself, and handed me one. "Screw those guys in the living room," he said. "Let's party. It's what Emily Cooke would have wanted."

The can was warm in my hand. Its silver-and-red label was familiar from commercials, but it was nothing I'd ever dared try before.

Or something Daytime Emily had never dared try. Cowering, fearful Daytime Emily, who never had any fun and who no one paid attention to. But that was not who I was anymore.

Pulling back the tab on the beer, I hit myself in the face with a spurt of frothy spray. "We wouldn't want to let Emily Cooke down." I licked the beer splatter off my lips, and then I tipped back the can and took my very first sip of beer.

It was disgusting.

You know how beer smells? Sort of like cat pee by way

of a heady, boozy stench? Combine that with a terrible bitter taste that lingers on the tongue, and a warm frothy bubbliness like a can of cola that's been left open in the sun for three weeks, and you can imagine maybe a fraction of the nastiness.

I could have just set the can aside—it's not like I had the need to prove myself to Dalton and his friends—but I wanted the thrill of doing something that, before this night, would have been totally forbidden to me. Drinking this was completely illegal. Totally immoral. If my dad knew I was out drinking, he'd probably break down into sobs and wonder how he failed me.

I guzzled the entire can without taking a breath, elated, feeling freer than even the night before. Slamming down the can, I crushed it with my hand as easily as Dalton had. The pots above my head quaked from the force of my smash.

The guys stared at me in awe for a second as the booze settled into my mostly empty stomach, making me feel half-queasy. Then they all laughed, and Dalton raised his hand high in the air. I looked at him in confusion, then got it—he wanted a high five. I slapped his hand with my own.

"Good one!" he shouted.

"Pass me another," I said.

He did and grabbed one for himself. At the count of three we downed the cans, slammed them on the counter, grabbed two more, and did it again.

After the fourth beer, my stomach definitely felt odd. My head felt strangely hollow and light, like it had filled with helium and was about to drift up toward the ceiling. I wobbled on my countertop perch. Everything was half-blurry and half much too clear, and every time someone spoke, it took me a moment to realize what was going on before snapping to attention and listening intently. Everything everyone said seemed the funniest thing I ever heard, and we all laughed uproariously.

Somehow I ended up scooted across the island, resting against Dalton's broad, muscular chest, just taking in his smell. His musk was so strangely familiar and reassuring, the lingering smell of his girl making me giggle to myself even as I caressed his arm. I was invading another girl's territory, and I loved every second of it.

"Dalton!"

The voice was shrill, the echo of it in the kitchen a buzz in my ear. Grimacing and sitting up, I saw a pair of shadowy figures in the doorway. Squinting, I made out Zach. Standing next to him was a conservatively dressed, pretty girl with long red hair.

Nikki Tate. Dalton's girlfriend.

Nikki gaped at us, her lips opening and closing as though she wasn't sure what to say. Beside her, Zach muttered, "Sorry, Nikki."

"Hey," Dalton slurred. I resumed stroking his arm. Nikki's nostrils flared.

"Dalton," she said again, her voice quiet now, though I could hear a quavering behind her practiced, calm tone. "Put down your beer. I'm taking you home."

Dalton gazed at her, his jaw slack. He blinked. "Huh? Why would I do that? I'm *thirstay.*"

"Put it *down*," Nikki repeated, her tone going shrill at the end. She raised her hand and clenched it into a fist, as though miming gripping the beer can. She jerked her hand down.

As if in response, the half-full can dropped from Dalton's hand against the counter, so forcefully it was as though Nikki had indeed yanked it from his grip. Beer spilled as it landed, and I felt the warm liquid seeping into the back of my jeans. With a yelp, I leaped down from the counter and away from Dalton.

Without another word, Nikki grabbed Dalton by the arm and tugged him toward the kitchen door. He protested, his words slurred and unintelligible.

Zach stood in the doorway, glaring at me. I felt the eyes of the other guys in the kitchen on me as well, and I could make out a few girls in the hallway watching.

Seemed they wanted a show. Well, they were going to get one. I chased after Dalton and grabbed him by the waistband of his jeans. He stopped, pulled free of Nikki, and turned to face me.

"Sorry your girl had to ruin our fun," I said loudly enough for everyone to hear. "Leave her at home next time."

With that, I stood on my tiptoes, stuck out my tongue, and licked the side of his face. To my amusement, he let out a titter.

For a long moment, Nikki stood still, her eyes narrowed. Quavering and red-faced, she pulled Dalton past Zach and into the hallway.

Everyone stood silently, watching me. My head woozy, my vision blurred, and feeling like I was about to fall over at any moment, I looked them all in the eye and smiled.

"What's everyone staring at?" I said, my voice as thick as if I was talking through a mouth full of cotton. "Let's party!"

Clutching a twelve-pack in one hand and an open beer in the other, I shoved my way into the hallway. My destination: the front room. Those people needed to stop crying about Emily Cooke and start having fun.

Stumbling, I pushed past a girl with black hair, muttering, "Watch it."

The girl gripped me by my upper arm and spun me to face her. I dropped the twelve-pack, and it landed against the wood floor with a metallic thump.

"Let go," I snapped. Then, blinking rapidly to clear the blur from my eyes, I realized there were *three* of the girl who'd grabbed me. I was seeing in triplicate. I laughed.

"What's so funny?" the black-haired girl on the right said. "You think getting all up on Nikki's boyfriend is hilarious?"

"I don't know what you're trying to prove, Emily Webb," the black-haired girl in the middle said, "but you better stay away from him."

The black-haired girl on the left stood silent and back away from the others, her eyes down.

I blinked again. They were still a trio.

"Whoa," I slurred. "There really are three of you."

That's when I recognized them. The ABC triplets: Amy, Brittany, and Casey Delgado. They used to all have identically cut, incredibly long, shiny black hair that hung to their butts, but apparently they'd all cut their hair in three different styles for the new school year.

The triplet in the middle—Amy, the one with the mole on her nose that could easily be confused with a black nose stud, whose hair hung manelike and wild over her shoulders—scowled at me. She stepped forward and shoved me in the shoulder.

"You hear us?" she said. "Don't mess with Nikki or you're going to have to mess with us."

Oh, no, she did *not* just shove me.

Wobbling slightly, I got in Amy's face. "Or you'll do what?" I snarled. "You think you can hurt me? Aren't you afraid you'll break a nail?"

Amy's nostrils flared. She was about to say something else when someone started shouting behind us.

I turned to see the front door wide open, Nikki and Dalton standing chest to chest on the porch and waving their arms. I couldn't make out what they were saying, but Dalton was the one shouting. He raised a hand, and for a moment it appeared that notoriously kind Dalton McKinney was going to smack a girl half his size. Instead he stormed off down the porch steps. Nikki chased after him.

The endlessly depressing dirge from the entertainment room finally shut off, and a group of the pretty people burst out to see what was up. Mikey Harris was in the lead, Spencer by his side, his head only coming up to Mikey's chest. He was so tiny, that kid.

My stomach roiled and anger at Amy Delgado burned in my chest, but all of that was forgotten when I smelled it. The scent. *His* scent.

Some distant voice spoke in my brain: *Find* this *smell. He's the one.*

And I saw him—the new guy, right behind Mikey and Spencer, crouched against the wall near the front door as though he was trying to hide in plain sight. But he couldn't hide from me. He might as well have had a glowing spotlight on him, looking so very hot in his tight black shirt with his dark hair mussed and gelled, his sharp brow furrowed. Forgetting all about the raging Latina triplets behind me, I took a sip from my beer and lurched down the hallway.

"Hey!" Mikey Harris called as I came toward him. "What's going on out here? I thought I made it clear that this party was sober. Who brought beer?"

A girl behind Mikey sniffed and brushed a tear from her eye. "That is *so* disrespectful to Emily."

"This whore was getting drunk and throwing herself at Dalton McKinney," one of the triplets called behind me.

"Yeah, she was all over him right in front of Nikki," another said.

I ignored them all. I didn't care what was going on, I just had to find the source of the musk, had to nuzzle the guy it belonged to. Patrick was all I could see through my foggy eyes. I tripped over my own feet and banged into the stairs, but I immediately righted myself and kept on walking.

Mikey stepped in front of me, blocking my way. I tried to move around him, but he stepped into my path.

"Hey, who are you? Why were you messing with Dalton?"

I grunted. "Me? He was the one drinking. I just joined

in. Seemed more fun than your little pity party in there." I gestured with my beer hand toward the open double doors leading to his TV room. Brown-yellow booze sloshed out of the can and onto Mikey's shirt.

"That doesn't sound like Dalton," Mikey said, so intent on grilling me that he didn't notice the new stain on his polo.

"It's true, man," a male voice said behind me. I spun around, a little too fast, and had to bounce off of the wall to keep my balance. The lights were way too bright in the foyer. Why did they make the lights so damn bright?

Zach stood there. I could barely make out a couple of the other football players peeking out of the kitchen doors, sheepish.

"Sorry, Mikey," Zach said. "It was Dalton's idea. We were just trying to loosen up. I know this was supposed to be to remember Emily Cooke and all, but we're all nerves after what happened . . ."

Quietly Mikey said, "Spence, go make sure that Dalton's not trying to drive, will ya?"

"Yeah," Spencer said, then turned to run off.

"And you," he said to me. "You come with anyone?"

I ignored his question and tried to shove past. He didn't budge.

"Move," I slurred. "I'm on a mission."

"You're drunk and I'm not letting you drive."

I tried to get past him again. "Thanks for the PSA," I said. "But I'm busy. Move."

This time, Mikey stepped forward, setting me off balance. I reached out to grab the banister. My beer slipped out of my hands, smacking against the hardwood floor and spilling.

"Seriously," he said. "I don't know who you are, but maybe we can call someone or—"

Rage burned inside me, an inferno in my gut. Lip raised into a sneer, I stood on my tiptoes and got in Mikey's face. "I go to your school," I said, jabbing a finger into his chest. "My name is Emily Webb. And you need to get out of my frickin' way!"

I was angry again, more angry than I'd ever been before. With a cry, I shoved Mikey in his chest.

And he flew.

Pinwheeling his arms like a cartoon character, Mikey tumbled backward from the force of my shove. He smacked against a guy behind him, and both of them fell against a bench near the front door.

Ignoring the outraged cries of the other party guests, I marched to where I'd seen Patrick, but the musky, perfect scent had faded. It was somewhere outside now, and there was no one by the wall near the front door.

Patrick had left.

"Good going, jerk," I slurred at Mikey where he lay stunned, sprawled half against the bench and half on the floor. "You made me lose him."

I stormed through the people who weren't quick enough to get out of my way, then stomped out into the night. The fat guy with the shaved head was still out there, and he tried to grab me.

"Lay off," I snapped, yanking my arm free from his stubby fingers.

I staggered across the lawn, my body seeming to fight me with every step. Smacking into a few parked cars, I lumbered into the darkened street. The smell led into the woods across from Mikey's house, the same woods that eventually ended near where I lived.

Distantly I heard two loud pops, like firecrackers going off, then the sound of a girl screaming.

Ignoring the screams, I walked into the trees. As I did, a strong, queasy pain struck. As much I wanted to keep going, to chase after Patrick's scent, I had to stop and bend over, one hand clutching my stomach and the other against the rough bark of a tree.

I didn't feel right. My body shivered, my insides swirled in my gut. My head felt like it was filling up with water, like my head was a sponge and I was soaking up the ocean. Above me, the stars in the moonless night glowed too terribly bright, burning into my eyes.

The confidence I'd felt all evening drained away, and the cold of night swelled over me.

I fell to my knees and gagged. The alcohol burned in my stomach. I needed it out of me. I gagged again. My whole body convulsed as I retched, then threw up.

It didn't help. My stomach still hurt, my vision was still blurry, my head still muddied. I stood and staggered away from the puddle of watery vomit. More pain lanced through my body—my fingers and toes throbbed as though they'd been pounded with a hammer. My skin prickled with goose-flesh, the fine hairs puckering like little needles jabbing my arms. And then the pain in my stomach burst, like someone had grabbed two big handfuls of flesh and torn me open.

Crying out, I fell to the soft ground, wet leaves sticking to my hair and mud staining my perfect green top. I didn't care, couldn't care. The world swirled around me as I huddled with my knees to my chest, trying to cry out as my body convulsed, feeling as though I'd been tossed in a blender with some sadistic madman pounding on the pulse button.

And then it was over. My brain was still off-kilter and hazy, but I felt . . . better.

The woods around me weren't quite as blurry any-more, but it seemed as though the color was leached from them, everything in shades of dark gray and black. I noticed things I hadn't before—the knothole in the tree in front of me, the rustling of some meek little animal in the bushes to my right, a man-shaped shadow to my left cast by no source that I could see. I snorted and sniffed, smelling the wet leaves, the sour scent of my vomit, the pee of some dog who'd been walked here exactly eight hours and thirty-seven minutes ago. And of course, I smelled *his* smell. His perfect, alluring scent.

I groaned deep in my throat, the sound coming out like a dog's growl, then tried to get to my feet. I immediately pitched forward onto my hands. My view was crystal clear, so I had no way to explain what I was seeing, but my arms looked like they were covered in smooth gray and black fur. My fingernails had grown long, sharp, and black; the weight of my body on my hands sank them into the soft earth.

On all fours, I started to stalk forward, then yelped. My legs felt bound with rope or something, so tightly that they hurt. Swiveling around, I reached down and slashed with my long nails. In a moment, my pants were shredded. They were barely clinging to me and still felt much too tight, but now at least I could move. And that was all that mattered.

Wobbly, I stood, then started walking forward. The scent was growing increasingly faint. I had to hurry.

The last thing I remember as I tore deeper and deeper

into the woods was the feeling that I was being watched. That same feeling from the night before of some *presence* hovering near me, observing me.

Only this time, I could see it. See *them*. All around me I saw more of the shadowy man-shaped figures, standing still, doing nothing. Only they weren't shadows, not really—more like human statues carved from the blackness around me, somehow seeming both weightless and horribly solid at the exact same time.

Though nothing else about the dark woods worried me—what could hurt *me*?—something about the shadows, about the way they stood so perfectly still, burned itself into my brain, grabbing hold of some sort of ancient fear and making me whimper.

I ran away from the shadows, toward the smell.

I remember absolutely nothing else.

The Vesper Company
"Envisioning the brightest stars, to lead our way."
- Internal Document, Do Not Reproduce -

Partial Transcript of the Interrogation of
Branch B's Vesper 1
Part 3—Recorded Oct. 31, 2010

F. Savage (FS): You can't remember anything else?
Vesper 1 (V1): Sorry. It was the beer. I guess I
blacked out.
FS: How unfortunate.
V1: Don't worry. It's not the last time it happens.
Not the blackout drinking! I kind of swore off
beer. I mean the changing.
FS: [laughs.] Oh, of course, I'm aware of everything
else that happens. But this is all quite fascinating
to read. The varying lengths of your mental shift
before the full-on transformation . . . so very
different from any other vesper I've had the chance
to study.
V1: So what is that, anyway? You keep calling me a
vesper, but you called us deviants earlier too.
FS: It's just a term for our records, Emily. Vespers
are . . . special. Precious to us in a way you can't

imagine. But you are different than the vespers I've worked with in the past. Like I said, the deviant nickname may be unfortunate, but it works for—

V1: The vespers you didn't observe.

FS: That's one way to phrase it. But that is why I find this so *interesting*. The progression of the change . . .

V1: Yeah. I thought about it, and I guess it was sort of like a car revving up after not being used for a while, you know? Like someone turned the key and it churned for a bit, then died. Turned again and it churned even longer. Turned the key one more time and . . .

FS: Then the engine turned over, and you transformed all the way. Wonderful!

V1: Oh yeah, it's totally a blast.

FS: Oh, please excuse my enthusiasm. I can sometimes be a bit, ah, excitable. Just ask my colleagues.

V1: I'll be sure to do that later around the water cooler.

FS: [laughs.] You have quite the sardonic sense of humor at times!

V1: Sorry. I guess it's hard not to be sarcastic under the circumstances.

FS: Yes, I suppose that's understandable. [clears throat] In any case, let's move back to this past chapter. Quite an eventful party. And interesting how many familiar names were there. It almost seems fated.

V1: Yeah, well, me beelining for Dalton wasn't much of a coincidence, but—

[V1 ceases to speak as another round of muffled

thuds and booms sounds. These noises are louder
than the ones indicated in previous transcript
(Part 2). Noises quickly cease.]
V1: Seriously, is everything all right out there?
FS: Must be. Yes, of course. If there were an is-
sue, I'd surely be contacted.
V1: If you say so.
FS: Hmm, well, I don't think we really need to go
into further detail on what we've just read. Let's
continue on.

THERE HAS TO BE A LOGICAL EXPLANATION

Lesson for the day, kids: Hangovers are real, and they are the opposite of fun.

I woke the next morning with sunlight slicing between my open curtains and stabbing my eyelids. I grimaced. My limbs, my back, my chest—every part of my body felt stiff, overworked. There was a constant throbbing pain in my forehead, and my mouth tasted like I'd spent last night licking a toilet.

Last night. Oh no, last night.

I sat up in bed and immediately regretted it. I still felt woozy, and my head seemed determined to roll off my neck. I forced open my crusted eyes. As usual, everything was blurry.

I fumbled for my glasses on my nightstand, then slipped them on.

The first thing I noticed: my pants. The nice, tight-fitting pants Dawn had let me borrow were torn to shreds, hanging from my hips like a denim hula skirt. At least the green tank she'd loaned me was fine. She'd probably start to notice soon if even more of her clothes began to disappear.

Everything in my room seemed in place, with the exception of the curtains, which had been left open, something I never do. Second story or not, I don't want anyone able to spy on me. I realized suddenly that I had no idea when or how I'd gotten up to my room the night before. I remembered me and Dalton in Mikey Harris's kitchen, I sort of remembered running off into the woods, getting sick, and . . .

"School," I muttered. "Oh man, it's a school day."

The clock told me it was 7:43 a.m. I was supposed to get picked up by Megan in fifteen minutes.

Stumbling only slightly, I made it across the hall to the bathroom. I suddenly really, really had to pee, but my mouth still tasted horrifying, and I seriously needed an aspirin or an ibuprofen or something else for my head. I popped the pill first, putting my head down and gulping at the water pouring from the faucet, then compromised on the other two problems by sitting on the toilet and brushing my teeth at the same time. I kicked off the pants as I sat down. No use wearing those anymore.

Finishing my business, I flushed, got up, and spat the toothpaste froth into the sink. It hadn't helped. The inside of my mouth still tasted like death.

It was then, standing over the sink and squinting at my own bleary, red-rimmed eyes in the mirror, that I remembered. I remembered Dalton, Nikki's angry face, the triplets promising to hurt me, tossing poor Mikey Harris aside, chasing after Patrick's smell, and . . .

Changing. I remembered *changing*.

"No way," I whispered, and turned away from my hideous reflection. What Crazy Emily had done was bad. Supremely bad. Girls like me just did not go to parties and make scenes like that, did not challenge the royalty of high school, did not shove one of their prized leaders. And they certainly didn't try to steal another girl's boyfriend. That was something people did only in nighttime soap operas. Heck, daytime soap operas too.

And what was all that about, anyway? What was my alter ego's freakish obsession with boys? Licking Dalton's face, following another one's scent—and that, too. The endless, irresistible urge to smell guys. It was like I'd transformed into a confident, kick-ass girl every night, but rather than be a superhero or something, I spent all my time trying to find a guy to pounce on.

What did that say about me? All this time I'd hidden in my room, reading my books, covering my, er, womanly attributes up so no one would ogle me. I didn't do anything at school, really, so let's face it: I had no idea what I wanted to do with my life. I mean, I had my fantasies about who I'd *like* to be—not careers, really, just the idea of becoming a woman who was strong and confident and utterly calm in any situation—but before the past few nights they were just wistful imaginings. Other girls fantasize about being something actually achievable, like lawyers or doctors or artists or models. Heck, even wanting to grow up and be a mom is a goal.

But without really knowing who I was, what I was meant to be, I never imagined that maybe the real reason I wished I was like the cool girls on TV was because I wanted to . . . get a boyfriend. Which didn't even make sense, because that had hardly ever been my lifelong goal, and besides, how pathetic is that? Not the wanting-to-date part—that was fine—but more that I guess some deep, dark, subconscious part of me apparently had *only* that as a goal. Dress up to get the boys. Act crazy to get the boys' attention. Lick the boys. Chase the boys.

Standing there in the bathroom, my feet bare against the cold tile, I didn't know what to think. Maybe my brain was still addled from the beer after all. I should have taken

Megan's advice the night before and tied myself up. Why hadn't I? Why, despite how disturbing it was to have these crazy mood swings, did a big part of me find Nighttime Emily kind of appealing, even with her penchant for acting like a contestant on a trashy reality dating show? Breaking rules. Getting in people's faces. That wasn't me, no matter how fun it felt at the time.

And that was the whole point, wasn't it? For all her many flaws, Nighttime Emily was the embodiment of every crazy fantasy I'd had since I started high school, given up Megan's dream of us becoming popular, and completed my transformation into a wallflower loner. Only Nighttime Emily apparently completely lacked any sense of social correctness.

I turned back to the sink and splashed water on my dirt-streaked face, then ran a brush through my hair before pulling it back. Even though I felt supremely grimy, there was no time for a shower. I snagged the ruined pants from the floor, ran back into my room, and tossed them into the closet.

There was no denying I'd gotten drunk last night. Supremely drunk. But was it possible to get so drunk that I'd hallucinated? I mean, blurry though my vision was, I had clearly seen my arms and hands. I remembered them being longer, covered in fur, my hands transformed into claws.

That wasn't possible, clearly. I mean, just 'cause I was some sort of were-slut, that didn't mean I was a . . .

Werewolf.

The word popped into my brain as I pulled on my jeans, and it felt so very right that I stopped with only one leg on. Falling back, I sat on my bed. I glimpsed Ein still lying on his back in the corner where I'd kicked him the night before.

A werewolf. What a crazy thing to hallucinate. Between that and the whole Emily Cooke spirit idea, maybe I'd just been watching too many horror movies. Combine that with booze . . .

But then, what about how when I was Nighttime Emily, I spent so much time *smelling* everything? How I was stronger, faster, graceful? What about how my vision miraculously cleared, and everything I heard and felt sizzled with intensity? Or how I'd somehow managed to tear my pants to shreds with just my hands, how there was dirt still stuck under my fingernails from where I clawed into the damp earth . . . ?

And let's face it: That explanation made a whole lot more sense than my theory that the other Emily had possessed me. Not that I had ever really taken that too seriously—

Well, maybe a little.

"There has to be a logical explanation," I said, then let out a bitter laugh at how I sounded like the scientist character

127

in every bad horror movie I'd ever seen once he's faced with something out of the norm. "No, seriously. Maybe I found . . . scissors or something in the woods. Maybe . . ."

I didn't know. I didn't have any answers.

It had to be a hallucination, I decided. Beyond the whole wolf-girl thing, I also remembered seeing and *feeling* ghostly, shadowy figures standing all around me.

Werewolves. And ghosts. All of that belonged strictly in the realm of fantasy. At least my change into someone with a bad case of the crazies could be explained rationally by a brain tumor or something.

Reassuring.

It was 8:05. Already five minutes past the time when Megan was normally outside honking at me. School started in fifteen minutes.

Oh man, all this time I'd been getting ready to go to the one place I probably should never go back to, ever again: Carver Senior High. Home of the Carver Cougars and all the pretty, important people I'd made a complete and utter spectacle of myself in front of the night before.

So here were my choices: feign sickness and stay at home all day, trapped in my room with nothing to do but think about last night all day long, or go to school, where I would have to suffer the wrath of the entire junior class.

Okay, maybe you'll think I'm even more nutso than you

already do, but I decided on school. It's just that, for the first time in my life, the idea of being trapped in a room filled with books, comics, and movies all about strange, supernatural happenings didn't sound all that appealing. I actually wanted normal, boring reality for once.

Besides, I was back to being glasses-wearing, makeup-less, hoodied Emily Webb. Maybe no one would recognize me.

Right.

I was halfway down the stairs to the living room when the front door slammed, and I heard my dad's stomping footsteps. He screamed out my name. "Emily? Emily!"

Confused, I peeked down the stairs and waved at him. "Yeah?" I said.

Relief washed over his face, and he put his hand to his chest. He was wearing his pajama bottoms with his sneakers on, and also his faded leather jacket. His glasses, as always, were crooked—had he been outside?

Before I could move, the door opened wider and Dawn rushed in, still wearing her clothes from last night, followed by my short stepmother.

That was when I finally remembered—I'd ditched Dawn last night. I was guessing I hadn't checked in with her before ending up in bed, either. My face flushed with embarrassment.

"Emily!" Dawn called at the sight of me. She raced up the stairs to pull me into a hug. "Oh, dude, I was so, so scared. I'm so glad you're fine."

"I'm sorry," I whispered. "I guess I got kinda drunk, and I wasn't thinking. . . ."

I couldn't say anything else because at that moment my dad and stepmom finally reached me, and they, too, drew me into a hug.

"I was worried out of my mind, Leelee," my dad said. I could hear it in his voice; he definitely wasn't lying. Oh, my poor dad! I'd never done anything like this, ever. How he must have felt . . .

"Sorry, Dad," I said, my voice muffled against his chest.

"You're in so much trouble, little girl," he said. "But oh, am I glad to see you."

My stepmother pulled away, her glasses wet with tears. A lump formed in my throat. She was such a nice woman, my stepmom, and here I'd gone and made her cry.

"I'm sorry, Katherine," I whispered to her.

She sniffed and took off her glasses to wipe at her eyes. "We heard about that boy getting shot, and I had this horrible feeling," she said between wipes. "I was so afraid that whoever is doing this . . ." She sobbed, and my dad let me go to put his arm around her.

For a moment, I thought she must have been confused

about the gender of Emily Cooke. Then I remembered another detail of my blurry evening: the popping sounds. The girl screaming.

"A boy was shot? Who?"

Dawn shook her head. "I don't know his name. Somebody at the party, though. A girl came screaming down the street after you ran off, saying we needed to call 911. . . ."

I couldn't breathe. There were three guys who I saw leave the party right before I did, but only one of them was with a girl. Trembling, I ran down the steps into the living room. Fumbling with the remote control, I flicked on the TV.

" . . . And now over to Nancy Smith, who is on location at Carver Senior High School in Skopamish, where another sixteen-year-old student has fallen victim to an unknown assailant."

I could sense my family crowding behind me, but they didn't say anything. I stood in front of the couch, so nervous that I couldn't sit down or even lower the hand that held the remote.

The image cut to a view of my high school. There were some students and teachers milling around out front, but far fewer than usual. The camera panned over to rest on a blond woman in a suit, standing in front of the stone Carver High sign with a microphone to her chin.

"A community is broken by fear this morning at the news that another bright young student has fallen victim to a crazed gunman."

A picture flashed on-screen: Dalton. Attractive, sweet-faced Dalton McKinney—who'd never said a bad word to anyone, but who'd acted totally opposite from his normal self last night, just like I had.

I gasped and put my hands to my face.

"Carver Senior High School football star Dalton McKinney is the latest victim of an assailant that police now believe to be the same person who killed fellow student Emily Cooke earlier this week."

"No," I whispered.

"Dalton McKinney is currently in Harborview Medical Center and listed in critical condition, though we were told just moments ago that doctors are hopeful for his survival. Fellow students and parents are at the hospital this morning waiting anxiously to learn if he'll be all right, and whether or not police will be able to find the person responsible for these attacks."

I clicked the TV off. Dalton was alive.

But he almost wasn't. He'd left the party early and ran into the killer for one reason and one reason only: me. If I hadn't acted the way I had, Nikki never would have become upset, Dalton never would have . . .

It was at that moment that the cautious pleasure I'd had from being Nighttime Emily went away completely. No matter how exciting she was, last night she'd taken it too far, and now I hated her, what she'd made me become, how she made me treat everyone around me.

I turned to Dawn. "The girl who ran back, is she okay?" I asked. "Was she hurt?"

Dawn grimaced as she remembered. "She seemed fine, but there was . . . uh, there was blood on her hands from trying to help that boy . . ."

"Did she say anything? Did she see who it was?"

Dawn shrugged. "I don't know, it was chaos. Everyone was still reeling from whatever happened with you downstairs, and then the girl ran back screaming that her boyfriend had been shot."

I didn't ask any more questions, but even as I stood there wobbling with shock, I had to wonder: Why did the killer only shoot Dalton? If he was going around killing random teens, why not Nikki, too? Or Spencer, if he'd managed to catch up with them?

Maybe the shootings weren't so random after all.

It was eight fifteen. School was about to start. Suddenly I didn't feel quite as gung ho about going.

10

I HEARD WHAT YOU DID

I was officially grounded.

I know in the grand scheme of things, especially considering all the insanity of the past few days, being grounded should have been the least of my problems. But here's the thing: I had never once been grounded in my entire life. I'd never done anything even remotely requiring a punishment of that magnitude. Doing grounding-worthy things usually requires a person to leave the house.

But drinking and wandering off and disappearing all night? Yeah, that was worthy of punishment, being forced to stay home with no internet or TV for the weekend. I wasn't mad at my dad or anything. I was glad he was laying down the law. I deserved it.

Oh, how my life was changing.

I wanted to stay home that day, just surround myself with my dad and stepmom and Dawn, even if they were going to spend the next several hours lecturing me on the dangers of alcohol and of acting so reckless. My dad was sympathetic at first, thinking maybe I wanted to go to the hospital along with all my "friends" and hold vigil, waiting to hear about Dalton. I refused and gave a lame excuse about being afraid of hospitals; I couldn't really explain why my showing up there would be the worst idea since George Lucas said, "Hey, how 'bout some prequels?"

Thinking I was trying to get out of my education on top of everything else, he forced me to go to school. I couldn't really blame him.

Megan wasn't outside when Dawn drove me to school. Of course not; school had started twenty minutes before. But a quick check of my cell phone showed that she also hadn't called me. After the frantic way she'd been all over my case the past few days—ever since seeing me transform into the type of girl she loathed with every fiber of her lanky being—and after hearing about Dalton, surely she would have checked up on me.

That she hadn't? I had no idea what it meant, but I had to assume with her it was because she was mad at me. Join the club, Reedy.

"Okay, so, I'll come here to pick you up right after school."

Dawn leaned against the steering wheel of her car, looking at me with a serious expression I'd never once seen from her. Grabbing my backpack from where it rested between my knees, I opened the door, then hesitated.

"I'm really sorry," I said without turning around.

For a moment, she didn't say anything. Finally she said, "I was really, really worried about you, dude."

"I know, I—"

"Just don't ever do that to me again. I want to help you break out of your shell and all, but not if it means you're going to make me think you're dead all night."

I turned to her. I smiled weakly. She did not return the expression.

"I won't. I promise."

She coughed and looked away. "All righty. So right after school, then. I need to go home and take a nap."

"Okay."

Clutching my bag to my chest, I surveyed the school. The brick buildings were quiet, seeming almost empty. The sky was a matte gray—it often was in the morning—and the cool wind blew through the towering evergreens that surrounded the school. Across the parking lot there were news vans, some preparing to pull away, others setting up cameras. The reporter from TV that morning talked with her cameraman, cradling a steaming cup of coffee and laughing.

Near the front doors was a pile of flowers and teddy bears, ribbons tied to the pole they rested against. Last year's school pictures of Emily C. and Dalton were pasted against the brick wall. They both looked so happy. At least maybe Dalton would get to take a new picture.

I went to the front office and gave the secretary the note my dad had written, and she wrote something in her ledger and sent me on my way. Behind her the principal stood with the vice principal, the two women nodding solemnly while speaking to a pair of men I assumed were detectives based on the badges clipped to their belts.

I took my time walking through the quiet, empty halls to my locker. First period was already halfway over, and the last thing I wanted was to walk in and have everyone's eyes on me.

Storing my backpack, I wandered past the lockers, past the half-empty classrooms where the kids who either weren't close to Dalton or whose parents weren't overprotective enough to keep them home sat, learning reading and writing and 'rithmetic. I stopped outside of room 113: Mr. Woods's English class. Megan's first period.

I don't know how long I stood there until the bell rang; I more or less zoned out, my back against the lockers by the door and eyes cast down at the green tile floor, my mind circling around the same things over and over. Finally the doors burst open and kids began pouring out. Megan was one of the first. She walked right past me.

"Hey," I said, reaching out to touch her arm.

She stiffened and spun around, ready to verbally smack down whoever had touched her. But her face softened—only slightly—when she saw it was me.

Dragging me away from the door so we wouldn't be caught up in the wake of chattering kids rushing into the hall, she put her head close to mine.

"I heard what you did," she said through clenched teeth.

Oh crap.

I looked away from her accusing gray eyes and bit my lip. "Uh, yeah, so what did you hear?"

"Enough," she said. "When someone like us makes a scene, word gets around fast. Even when one of their lunk-head boyfriends almost gets murdered, people still have plenty of time to make comments online all night laughing about you getting smashed and acting like a whore."

I glanced sidelong at the kids passing us as they went to their lockers and classes. A few glowered at me, their expressions judgmental, before whispering into the ears of whoever they walked with.

I didn't know what to say. I stood silent, then finally said, "Dalton isn't a lunkhead. He's a nice guy."

Megan threw her hands in the air. "You're trying to become one of them, aren't you?" she said. "Is that what this is all about? You're pretending to have some sort of brain malfunction so, what, I wouldn't be mad that I'm not good enough for you anymore? Is that it?"

She crossed her arms and slammed back against the locker. Her lower lip trembled.

"What?" I said. "No! Of course not!"

"Right," she muttered. "Whatever."

We stood there in silence for a few moments. More kids walked by, their eyes melting holes in my hoodie. I turned away, faced the lockers, my cheeks burning.

"I promise you," I whispered, "I'm not trying to ditch you, and I'm not going to turn into a Sarah Plainsworth. I would never go all Heather on you like that."

Megan looked at me blankly. "Go all what?"

"You know, a Heather?" I said. "Like in the movie *Heathers*?"

Megan's look remained blank.

"Oh, we need to Netflix that, it's totally eighties and raunchy and great. There's evil popular girls dying left and right, you'd totally love it." The words left my mouth before I really thought about them—movies about dead popular girls probably weren't the best thing to talk about—and I winced.

Seemingly despite herself, Megan smirked and let out a sharp laugh. "Yeah," she said. "You always know what I'll love."

We stood there in silence. The first bell for next period rang, and the hall began to empty.

"Look," I said. "Something weird is going on with

me lately, I know. Maybe . . . maybe you could come over tonight, like you were going to do last night. When I start acting strange, you can make sure I don't run out and embarrass myself, or get myself shot."

"Your dad will be cool with that?" Megan asked me.

"Uh," I said. "I'm sort of grounded. But we'll see."

Megan's eyes went wide. "*You're* grounded?"

The second bell rang. The hall was completely empty.

"Oh crap," I muttered. "The last thing I need is detention." Rushing down the hall toward my class, I waved at Megan. "I'll tell you about it later," I said. "Just make sure your mom doesn't keep you home this time!"

Megan waved and ran off to her own class. I was completely unsure if I was doing the right thing by asking her to guard-dog me, but I knew I probably needed her now more than ever if I had any hope of keeping from wreaking havoc as Nighttime Emily. Or getting drunk and turning into . . .

I didn't want to think about it. I skidded around a corner and ran to Mr. Philbrick's biology class.

I opened the door as quietly as I could. Mr. Philbrick's expansive back was turned to me, and I peeked around him at the classroom. The first person I saw was someone I seriously did not expect to see at school that day: Amy Delgado.

She caught my eye just as I caught hers. She slowly mouthed, *Whore.*

I quietly shut the door. Guess there would be no science for me.

I ended up in the library, sitting on the short carpet, hiding behind the stacks. I wanted to cry, but that felt so stupidly childish. Yet why shouldn't I cry? I mean, I went from being completely anonymous to being called the "fat" Emily and the "whore" Emily, and Megan thought I was trying to drop her as a friend, and my whole family was mad at me, and because of me poor Dalton got shot, and there were my nighttime changes that had gone from being heady thrills to something completely out of control. . . .

My eyes burned with tears, but I refused to let them fall. What would Nighttime Emily do? She would stomp into biology class like she owned the place, call Amy Delgado a whore right back, prop her feet on her desk, and get good and ready for some book learnin'. She'd tell Megan to stop acting all oversensitive and start being more supportive, like a best friend should be.

Then she'd probably steal a car and go on a joyride down the freeway, maybe try to rob a bank to catch the attention of a cute guard.

I laughed to myself. My life was rapidly becoming ridiculous.

Grabbing the shelves, I hauled myself to my feet. I read the title on the spine of the book in front of me: *Werewolves, Witches, and Wandering Spirits: Traditional*

Belief & Folklore in Early Modern Europe.

Well, that was a freaky coincidence.

I hesitated for a moment, then grabbed the book off the shelf. There were a few more on similar subjects near it. I grabbed those, too.

Finding a table in the mostly empty, quiet lobby of the library, I sat down with my pile of books and began flipping through the pages. There were reproduced engravings of werewolves rampaging through villages, eating pigs and chickens and the occasional unlucky human. There was the standard talk about werewolf lore, you know the drill: turned into one after being bitten by another person cursed with lycanthropy, transforming with the full moon, killed only by silver bullets.

Well, none of that applied to me. The moon wasn't in the sky at all last night, and I'd certainly never been bitten by anyone, let alone a wolf. That's the kind of thing you'd remember. And I don't really want to test the theory, but I'm pretty sure that any bullet would get me good and dead, silver or no. That's what happened to Emily Cooke, at least.

I slammed shut the book and slumped onto my arms. This was completely stupid. Werewolves don't exist! They're just fodder for movies and books, and besides, how could someone completely transform into another creature in the course of a few minutes? It didn't make any sense. I had gotten drunker than a gutter bum the night before, that was all.

Maybe *all* people saw things when they got drunk. I mean, why else would people talk about "beer goggles"?

Sensing something, I glanced up. The librarian, a skinny woman with short white hair and wire-rimmed glasses, sat quietly at her desk, typing at a computer. I then realized that another student had come into the library while I'd had my nose in my book.

Patrick.

He sat across the lobby at another table, facing me but engrossed in whatever it was he was reading.

I remembered the musk that had made me feel all fluttery at lunch the other day, the way I'd gone all boy crazy when I smelled it at the party last night, frantically chasing him through the woods. I couldn't smell him from this far away, of course, but the memory of his scent had burned its message into some part of my brain that even Nighttime Emily had found strange: *He's the one.*

The one what?

I had to get up, go talk to him. He was new, and right around the time he appeared, all of this epic weirdness began. And something about him, some pheromone or whatever, drove me even crazier than I already was at night. Maybe he knew something about what was happening to me. Maybe . . .

I didn't move. I held a book in front of my face so he

wouldn't see who I was, peeking over the top so that I could watch him. Every few minutes I tried to psych myself up to go talk to him. *What would Nighttime Emily do?* I asked myself. But it didn't work. Because I wasn't Nighttime Emily. I was just me, Emily Webb, average, everyday geek who didn't have a courageous bone in her body.

Eventually he set down the book he was reading, grabbed his backpack, and left. I watched his tall form head toward the door, telling myself, *This is your last chance. Go talk to him.*

But I sat where I was, and then he was gone.

Feeling defeated, I grabbed the werewolf books and took them to the librarian to get checked out. That done, I headed toward the door myself—it was almost time for third period. Maybe I could sneak into class without anyone else noticing me.

As I passed the table where Patrick had sat, I glimpsed the book he'd been reading and had left behind. It was a large, black-covered book. Bold white letters read: *Serial Killers in America: Inside the Mind of Fear Itself.*

Well. That was . . . interesting.

Not sure what to think about Patrick's choice in reading material, and still cursing myself over my complete inability to suck it up and talk to a boy, I headed off to face the rest of the school day.

11

THE EMILY AND MEGAN MILKSHAKE SPECTACULAR

It was Friday night. Time for everyone to celebrate the end of their first week back at school by getting down, getting funky, getting their party on.

That is, everyone who wasn't currently preparing for the weekend funeral of a girl who'd died earlier in the week, or who wasn't at a hospital waiting to hear about the condition of a boy who'd been shot, or who wasn't cowering at home, afraid to go out because there was some crazy killer on the loose blowing away teenagers at random.

Or, if you were me, who never had a party to go to on a Friday night anyway but who was so grounded that even if I did, it was definitely a no-go.

I love my dad, but I'll say this about him: Sometimes he

can be completely clueless about how to be a parent. Most parents, upon discovering that their child had been out all night drinking, wouldn't be inclined to let them have a friend stay over the following night, even under the guise of said friend coming to keep an eye on me. They also wouldn't relent on the TV restriction, saying that they didn't want their child's friend to be bored, and they probably wouldn't go out and leave their child home all alone.

But I can't blame my dad too much. In all my sixteen years, he'd never had to worry about punishing me. And I was his little girl; no matter how angry and betrayed he'd felt, I guess I was easy to forgive. I assume that my step-mother tried to explain to him how to correctly raise a teenage girl, but I'll also say this about my dad: He can be incredibly stubborn when he wants to be.

That was how Megan and I ended up alone at my house that Friday night, in my living room watching a horror movie from twenty years ago. Dad and Katherine already had plans for the evening long before my wild display at Mikey Harris's party. Dawn, being an attractive young college student, was also out, shedding the usual jeans and casual tops she wore to school and working the crazy clubbing outfits I always ended up stealing whenever Nighttime Emily took over.

It's funny, but for some reason all three of them seemed

to trust me not to act out again that night. If only they'd known I didn't really have much of a choice.

"This movie is horrible," Megan declared, legs curled up under her on the couch. She grabbed the remote and flicked off the DVD. I didn't try to stop her. I was distracted and not really paying attention to the movie anyway, but what I had seen of it was, indeed, horrible. We had better gore effects in the homemade movie Megan and I had made when we were twelve—I'd played the monster slayer, and she'd played the monster.

It was only seven forty-five. Still a half hour to go before I transformed into Nighttime Emily and Megan would have to strap me to a gurney, or whatever it was she planned to do to keep me from going out.

"So what do you want to do now?" I asked. "We could watch another movie, but we've seen them all . . . maybe a musical, get singtastic . . ."

Megan shrugged. "I don't feel like singing. We've only got a half an hour to go until your supposed 'change' anyway." She flicked through channels until we ended up on a rerun of Ms. Nguyen's talk show. Megan chuckled and kept it on, while Ms. Nguyen—dressed in a teal pantsuit—chatted away in Vietnamese, presumably about a grainy still image of a UFO that was in the top left corner of the screen.

"I know," she said, muting Ms. Nguyen and turning to

face me on the couch. "Want to hear what Lucas told me earlier? About Emily C. and Dalton?"

I hesitated, then said, "What about them?"

"Well, Deputy Jared made photocopies of the police reports. Total inside knowledge about what went down."

I blinked. "Yeah, uh, that's sort of morbid."

Megan shrugged and buried herself back into the cushions. She swirled her finger over the armrest. "Well, you know how they said Emily C. was walking alone dressed only in flannel pajamas? How she didn't even have any shoes on? She walked, like, three miles barefoot. What they didn't say is that she cut her foot three blocks before where she died, that she had a big gash on her heel. The forensics people said from the tracks she made that it was like she didn't even notice, just kept on strolling, leaving a bloody trail. After her parents said she had been acting strangely that night, they tested her blood and, get this, she wasn't on drugs or drunk or anything either."

I shuddered, imagining it: Lithe, beautiful Emily Cooke walking trancelike down a dark street, her blond hair flowing behind her in the breeze, ghostlike. In her wake, a dark trail of red footprints staining the sidewalk . . .

I remembered Emily Cooke's stories, her photos, the funny notes she'd written to her friends. Imagining the way she'd been in her last moments bothered me, and I wasn't entirely sure why.

"Megan," I whispered.

She ignored me and kept talking, waving her hands animatedly as she described the scene. She was more excited and interested than I'd seen her in a long time.

"Then the killer shot her. No struggle, nothing. He must have just stepped in front of her, raised the gun, and *bam, bam*—shot her once in the chest, once in the neck."

"That's horrible." I wanted to tell her to stop, but part of me needed to hear this, how it went down. I hadn't really thought about it before, but maybe Emily Cooke had changed the same way I had—had longed for thrills so much that she hadn't even bothered getting dressed before running around outdoors. That would explain why she'd seemed erratic to her parents, how she was able to walk so far without shoes.

But I was pretty sure that even as Nighttime Emily I would have felt a cut on my foot and stopped to take care of it. So what did that mean about Emily Cooke? What was different about her situation?

Shifting so that she sat on her other leg, Megan went on. "And Dalton—well, you were there. They said he had some crazy high alcohol level, but his friends told police he was acting crazy even before he started drinking."

Like I had.

"They interviewed Nikki," she went on. "You know, that snotty cheerleader?"

"She's not . . ." I stopped myself. "Yeah, I know her."

Megan snorted a laugh. "Yeah, of course you do. With the face-licking thing." Snorting again, she continued. "Anyway, they were arguing, she said, then he started walking down the street and she chased after him. Some guy stepped in front of them, said something to Dalton, and shot."

I pictured it: the perfect high school couple, alone under a streetlight, Nikki worried about her boyfriend, and Dalton not afraid of anything. A dark figure appearing before them, talking in a low tone, raising a gun . . .

"How did Dalton survive?" I asked. "The report, did it say his injuries or anything?"

Megan nodded. "The guy shot once and Dalton raised his arm, got shot there. The guy shot again at Dalton's head. It hit one lobe of one hemisphere or something like that, but since most of the brain survived and he was responsive, they think he'll maybe be okay. I Googled it and only like five percent of people survive being shot in the head. He's lucky."

"Yeah," I whispered. "Super lucky."

Megan leaned back and once again swirled her finger over the armrest. "Well, anyway, Nikki said that after that the guy didn't even pay attention to her despite her screaming. He just turned and walked away."

So both Emily C. and Dalton were acting different from their normal selves those nights. And both of them ended up getting shot—by a guy who *ignored* Nikki Tate, who seemed to act the same way she always did.

Maybe they hadn't had the exact same intensely crazy change that I suffered at night, but still, they *had* changed. Somehow, someone out there knew this about them. And he'd hunted them down.

So what did that mean for me?

Something triggered in my brain then. Some hazy memory from the party the night before.

"Did the police report have a description of the killer?" I asked Megan. "Did Nikki get a good look?"

"Sort of," Megan said. "She couldn't see his face. She said he was wearing some long coat and a hat that hid his features."

And I remembered reaching Mikey Harris's house, waiting for Dawn to park the car. I remembered the strange guy dressed like he'd stepped out of a noir film, who somehow knew my name and started to ask me some question.

It was the killer. It had to be. He'd meant to shoot *me*, not Dalton, but when I got dragged away he switched targets.

Which meant I was right. Whatever made me, Emily C., and Dalton different meant that someone wanted us dead.

I didn't know what to say or do. I suddenly didn't feel at all safe alone in my house with only Megan to protect me. Turning around in my seat, I peeked behind us. The foyer was dark save for the blinking blue and green buttons on my dad's computer. The dining room and the kitchen beyond were almost pitch-black, despite the pale light streaming through the curtains, and the sky outside was just about completely dark. In fact, the only light on at all was a single lamp in the living room where we sat, casting long shadows in the corners.

"Boo," Megan said.

I jumped, then reached over and smacked her. "Stop it." I shivered, my mind racing. "Those stories are freaky."

Megan rolled her eyes. "Whatever, some people got shot, they'll catch the guy, life moves on. Besides, hello, we were just watching a horror movie. Your skittishness about all this is weird. You and your dad were dressing up like Laurie Strode and Michael Myers when you were in diapers."

The full impact of what had almost happened to me the night before hit me then, and I began to shake. Someone had shot Dalton. Someone had *meant* to shoot me.

"Megan," I said, standing up from the couch. "Megan, we need to call the—"

I gasped and clutched my stomach. Pain tore through

my midsection as I reached out for the coffee table, and I missed and fell to the rug. Twitching and jerking, I clenched my teeth, my fingernails tearing through my shirt and into the flesh of my stomach.

Megan was at my side immediately. "Is it happening?" she asked. "The change?"

I tried to speak, but all that came out of my mouth was a wheeze.

Straightening up, Megan began to back away. "Okay, well, this is real," she said, her voice wavering. "Okay, okay . . ."

But then, with one last gasp, it was over. I lay on the floor for a moment, looking up at the blinking digital clock on the DVD player. It was only 8:04.

Plenty of time to make the most of my Friday night.

Noticing I'd stopped convulsing, Megan kneeled down beside me. "Are you all right?" she asked. "Is it over?"

I answered her with a groan and by stretching out my arms and legs. She stepped back, and I considered kicking myself up to stand. But that was something my daytime self wasn't even remotely capable of doing. And hinting that I wasn't the same girl I'd been a minute ago wouldn't help my plans at all.

Instead I reached out and said, "Can you give me a hand up?"

Megan grabbed my outstretched arm and hauled me to my feet. The rug was plush beneath my toes, so I wiggled them, enjoying the tickling sensation. I felt more alive than I had before. I could feel the currents of the air against my bare arms as it coursed out of the AC vents, could smell the lingering scent of pot roast from the kitchen. I flicked off my glasses and the living room was crisp and clear, brighter than it had been moments ago even with only the lone lamp on in the corner. I could make out everything—the scuff marks on the floor from when we'd moved the couch last summer, the little stars I'd scratched into the entertainment center when I was ten and thought it needed some sprucing up, the hairline cracks in the glass coffee table that no normal person would be able to see without a magnifying glass.

My body coursed with all these sensations, my muscles felt taut, my arms and legs limber. I wasn't slouchy and lethargic anymore. I was pretty, I was strong, I was graceful.

And I was wasting it by being stuck in my house with big-nosed, bitter, boring Megan Reed.

"Emily?" she asked. "Are you okay?"

I snapped to attention, then smiled as I caught her concerned eyes. "Yeah, I'm good, no worries. I had the change spasm, but I feel . . . normal? I guess whatever it is isn't as strong anymore."

Megan didn't stop studying my face. "You're sure?" she

asked. "You don't have any desire to dress trashy and go streetwalking?"

Picking up my glasses, I slipped them on. The room went blurry, and I laughed. "I'm positive."

Megan was silent for a long time. "I don't believe you," she said at last. "You're way too twitchy."

I waved my hand dismissively and plopped down on the couch. "I'm just so *relieved*. Maybe I was just temporarily sick, y'know? That's a good thing!"

"Yeah . . ." Megan's eyes didn't move from me as she sat down stiffly on the couch, her arms crossed.

"What?" I asked. "Don't believe me? Want to tie me up or something? That's totally kinky, Reedy."

She slunk lower into the couch. "Fine, whatever, Em. Say I do believe you. What do you want to do now, then?"

What I wanted to do was to get out of this house and have fun. And though some voice was screaming in the back of my head that someone wanted to kill me, that I needed to stay put and hide, I ignored it. Instead I thought of a plan to get Megan out of the way and, ahem, *borrow* her car.

"Hmm," I said to Megan. "I'm thinking . . . *Scream* movie marathon. Since you're so into pretty teenagers getting murdered all of a sudden, and after those police stories I feel like rooting for Sidney Prescott. Oh!" I sat straight up. "You know what we haven't made in a long time? The

155

Emily and Megan Milkshake Spectacular."

"Yeah . . . ," she said again, then grinned. "Nothing like horror movies and milkshakes."

I leaped up from my chair. "Okay, you go get them started, I need to go pee. Back in a sec."

Before she could protest, I raced up the stairs, ran into the bathroom, and shut the door. I took my glasses off, then regarded myself in the mirror. I looked so plain. Sticking out my tongue at the image of Daytime Emily staring back at me, I turned on the faucet, then proceeded to dig through the medicine cabinet above the sink.

There. My stepmother's prescription sleeping pills. Palming several, I put the pill bottle back in place, flushed the toilet, and turned off the faucet. With glasses back on my face, I opened the bathroom door. Megan stood there, hands on her waist and tapping her foot.

"Whoa," I said. "Don't scare me like that."

She looked me up and down, then glanced over my shoulder into the bathroom. Narrowing her eyes suspiciously, she let me pass her, then followed me down the stairs and into the kitchen.

I grabbed the tub of vanilla ice cream from the freezer, setting it on the kitchen counter next to the blender along with the jug of milk, the bag of sugar, and the little bottle of vanilla extract. I gritted my teeth as I did all this, while

Megan gathered utensils from the drawers so we could scoop and measure. I glanced at the clock. It was almost eight thirty. Playing Martha Stewart was the last thing I wanted to be doing right now.

I tried to focus on the task at hand, forcing laughter and making geeky jokes with Megan as we put the ingredients in the blender and made our milkshakes. She poured the resulting beverage into tall glasses, and I went to the fridge to grab the chocolate syrup. I poured the syrup into the glasses, tightening my fist and using my super-handy night-time strength to crush the handful of pills clutched in my palm. While Megan went to put the ice cream back in the freezer, I sprinkled the pill dust into her milkshake, then stirred it together with the syrup.

"Here you go." I handed Megan the sleeping-pill-laced cup with a sweet smile.

She took a sip. "Awesome," she said. "Now let's get to the movie."

It took another half an hour of doing my best impression of Daytime Emily before Megan finally became drowsy and, mercifully, fell asleep. Her empty glass sat on the coffee table, a little puddle of spilled milkshake leaving an unsightly ring. Megan let out a honking snore while on the TV Neve Campbell chatted breezily on the phone with the ghost-faced killer for the first time. I shut the TV off just as the killer leaped out of a closet, cutting Neve off midscream.

Despite having a body like a bundle of twigs, Megan wasn't exactly light. But I lifted her in my arms with ease, carried her up to my room, and buried her under the covers on my bed. Leaving her sleeping there, I went to Dawn's room, raided her closet, and got dressed in the bathroom as quickly as I could.

"There," I said, as I lowered the mascara wand. I was dressed in this slinky, sparkly blue dress that ended at my upper thigh. This time I stole Dawn's black heels to go with it. My hair hung wavy to my shoulders, and my face was done up just the way Dawn had showed me before the party the day before.

I looked fan-freakin'-tastic. Much improved from my previous forays into the world of dressing to impress.

The urges from my unknown self swirled together with my own desires to head out and do something crazy: Party. Dominate. Find a guy. Find *the* guy.

Do something I had never before been brave enough to do.

Down the stairs I went. Megan's purse was on the dining room table where she'd left it. Reaching in, I dug through crumpled-up tissues and her unopened pads until I found her car keys.

It was time for me to take my show on the road.

12

CALL ME MISS WEBB

No matter how made up I was, it was difficult to seem glamorous driving Little Rusty—Megan's tiny, boxy car was white trash supreme. It was all I had, but driving up I-5 to Seattle, with the window down to air out the car's weird smells, modern cars zipping past, was completely annoying. Despite how good it felt to have the wind rushing through my hair.

The clock on the car's ancient radio read 9:23 by the time the highway curved to reveal Seattle's skyline: The stadiums lit up, Qwest Field glowing blue and gold. The Space Needle with its little blinking light on top. Skyscrapers to the right and the glittering water of Puget Sound off to the left, past the docks.

Skopamish was small beans compared to the big city. For how close I lived, I'd only ever been up to Seattle a few times in my life. Despite being Washington natives, my dad and I had done stupid, touristy crap like head to Pioneer Square with its twenty-foot-tall totem pole standing sentry before taking the Underground Tour, or ogling the fishmongers at Pike Place Market, after which I dragged my dad down to the comic-book store on the second level. There were school trips to the Pacific Science Center at the base of the Space Needle, and one time my dad made me go with him to a gaming con at the convention center downtown.

Fun times for easily amused children and old people wearing fanny packs, I'm sure. But Seattle isn't just famous for its coffee. It's also famous for its music, its hip twenty-somethings stalking the streets at night, having a good time.

Part of me wanted to turn around, head back to Skopamish to hunt down Patrick and his oh-so-right smell. But I resisted the urge. I'd done the high school thing, and it had been fun. But I longed for more. I had so much to make up for after all the years of doing *nothing*. Sneaking into adults-only clubs was a time-honored teen tradition—and now it was my turn.

I wasn't exactly sure where to go—I'd been in such a rush to leave that I hadn't bothered researching any clubs first. But I remembered the time Megan took me with her to the Art Institute of Seattle so she could sign up for some four-day workshop thing, and I recalled a club near there, nestled underneath the ancient viaduct that ran parallel to the water and right beside downtown. At the last second I saw the exit we'd taken, and I swerved into the right lane. Bright white headlights flared through the back window, reflecting off the rearview mirror and momentarily blinding me. The car behind me honked.

I honked right back, Megan's car making a pitiful gasping beep that would put fear into no man's chest.

The exit took me around an S-turn, dropping me off by the stadiums. Struggling to remember the route we'd taken, I took a few right turns until I somehow ended up on the viaduct and finally knew where I was.

And there it was. The club.

It was next to the off-ramp, beneath a bridge that led who knows where. The place was tinier than I remembered, but there was a line of attractive people out front and it had a cool sign: a close-up of a black-and-white-striped tiger, fangs bared.

The name of the place: Frenzy. I didn't know a thing about this club, but I didn't care—the name alone was enough for me to know this was exactly where I wanted to be.

There was a pay parking lot next to the club. I didn't have any money on me, so I didn't bother putting anything into the cash box by the street. Clutching the car keys, I strode past the people waiting in line on the sidewalk and cut in front of a pair of college-age guys. I stood in front of the doorman and flashed him a sly smile. Through the dark open doorway I could see flashing lights and hear the *thumpa-thumpa-thumpa* of dance music.

"Hey there, can I come in?"

The door guy was a Schwarzenegger clone—tall, bulging chest, square face, military haircut. His nose was smashed like he'd been punched in the face a few times. He scanned me over, then crossed his arms. His giant biceps seemed about ready to tear apart the sleeves of his black T-shirt.

"ID and cover," he said to me. He had a nice, deep Vin Diesel voice.

I widened my eyes and formed my lips into a surprised O. "I totally forgot my bag in my car. You wouldn't make me walk all the way back to get it, would you?" He seemed the type to want to rescue a damsel in distress, so I scrunched in on myself, trying to come off all frail and helpless.

His expression didn't change. He pointed to a sign on the door. "ID and cover or no getting in. No exceptions."

"Hey, man," one of the guys behind me said. "Look at her, she's old enough. I'll pay her cover, it's cool."

I turned around and smiled at the guy. He was tall and

lanky, his black hair whooshed up into a fauxhawk. He was smoking a cigarette, blowing the smoke up into the night sky. His friend next to him was shorter, his hair close-cropped, his tight shirt showing off an awesome body.

"Thanks, guys." Turning back to the bouncer, I patted his chest and started to walk in.

The bouncer put his arm out, blocking my way. "No ID, no entry. No—"

"—exceptions," I snapped. "I got it."

"Hurry up," a woman in the back of the line called. "It's cold out here."

I flashed the bouncer a smile. "Well, I guess I'll just have to go back and get my bag then."

The bouncer didn't say anything. Just stared at me, stone-faced.

I wanted to shove him aside, make him fall on his butt. I knew I could do it too. But I didn't want to call that kind of attention to myself—not yet, anyway.

I sauntered away down the sidewalk. As I passed, Fauxhawk brushed his hand against my arm. While his buddy showed his ID and paid the cover charge, Fauxhawk tossed his cigarette to the ground and stamped it out.

"Hey, I'll see you inside," he said. "I'm Blaze. You're . . . ?"

I leaned in close and sniffed him. Cheap cologne and

cigarettes. That other part of my mind whispered, *Not the one.* I shoved it back, once again resisting the urge to go back to the car, head home, and find the *right* guy.

"Call me Miss Webb," I said. "And I'd better see you on the dance floor."

Smirking, he handed his ID and a twenty-dollar bill to the bouncer. "Don't keep me waiting," he said.

He disappeared inside, and I dropped my smile. Getting in was supposed to be simple. I rounded the corner into the parking lot. I didn't have an ID or any money, of course. I was going to have to get creative.

I wandered around the base of the club, trying to find some other way inside. The wall facing the parking lot was featureless save for a giant billboard. I ended up in back of the building, in an alley. A green Dumpster lay open, stinking of spoiled meat and alcohol.

But there was something else back there: a fire escape.

Holding Megan's car keys in my teeth, I spread my heeled feet apart, bunched my legs, felt my thigh muscles wind tight like a spring.

And I leaped.

I don't know how high I jumped—a story, at least, so maybe fifteen feet. All I know is that it was as close to flying as I'd come, and the rush of wind through my hair, the feeling of liquid lightness, made my mind giddy. Then skin met steel, and I caught the rusted grating at the bottom of the catwalk, the thin strips of metal cutting into my fingers. Tensing my arms, I swung myself up over the railing and onto the fire escape. My heels dropped through the open grating, but I kept my balance.

From there it was easy going—stairs led up the next few stories to the roof. I clambered up them, the steps quaking beneath me and my shoes clanging loudly. The distant *thumpa-thumpa-thumpa* of the music seeped through the walls.

Finally I reached the roof. I climbed a little ladder, pulled myself over the small brick wall, and found myself in the middle of some sort of private party. There were couches up there, fashionable yellow-patterned love seats and high-backed wicker chairs. I saw a pair of women, one with a boyish haircut and the other with a long braid, cuddling up in one of the love seats, murmuring sweet nothings in each other's ears while taking sips from glasses filled with some sort of neon blue alcoholic beverage. On an opposite seat, beneath a tall potted fern that shaded them from the yellow spotlights, a man and a woman made out and groped each other. I could smell the lust wafting off them.

Ignoring the two couples, I strode to the door leading inside the club. The short-haired woman gave me an appreciative leer as I passed, before a scowl from her date sent her back to murmuring sweet nothings.

Finally I was in.

Immediately the music enveloped me, the *thumpa-thumpa-thumpa* joined with a bright swirl of electronic notes and a wailing vocal. I followed a stylish spiral staircase down to the floor below. The place was packed, men in formfitting shirts sprawled on couches next to women in outfits even more garish and revealing than my own. Whoever wasn't sitting was standing where they could find room, and everyone huddled together to talk and laugh. The music was so loud that I couldn't hear a thing anyone was saying. I saw a flight of stairs against the front wall leading to the ground floor.

Taking the keys from my teeth and clenching them in my hand, I shoved through the milling twentysomethings, catching snippets of conversations, smelling the alcohol on their breaths. They gave off such heat, these people—their bodies radiated with sexual tension.

Their energy was amazing, intoxicating. I could feel it seep into my pores, soaking into my blood. But there was something off about it. I knew I needed companionship, needed to be surrounded by others—but a new urge called out from the deep recesses of my brain that I hadn't fully explored. *Hide from these*, it said. *Find your fellows.*

The thought didn't make any sense. I bumped into

dancing, laughing people, and I felt like this *must* be the place I needed to be, even if that stupid, instinct-driven side of me tried to say otherwise. I felt like I was constantly sniffing and searching for someone—or maybe it was several someones—who my body would decide fit me perfectly. That night I was irritated by that side, refused to give into it. Why couldn't it just leave me alone and let me be happy with whoever I decided for myself was "the one"?

Again, I shoved down the urges. Winding past the people milling on the stairs, I finally made it to the ground floor. If I thought the place had been crowded upstairs, downstairs was even worse—people were everywhere on the dance floor, grinding against one another and raising their arms into the air, stomping to the beat of the music. Well, some of them were, anyway. Others had a serious case of White People Dancing Syndrome and shuffled along as though they were hearing a completely different song.

How anyone danced at all I didn't know, because they were packed in so tight that they seemed to become one large, writhing mass of sweaty flesh. In the center of the dance floor two chubby girls danced around poles on a little platform, the DJ at his turntable behind them. Their girlfriends and some guys whooped it up as the two made a spectacle of themselves, with no one seeming to remotely care.

I sniffed the air—over the smell of sweat, of hormones, and of booze, the cheap cologne and cigarette smoke of Fauxhawk stood out. From my vantage point on the stairs, I caught sight of him. He sat at the bar on the opposite side of the room, sipping a clear drink that could have been water but most certainly wasn't, while his crop-haired friend occupied himself with a girl on his lap.

I shoved through the dancers. No one seemed to care in the least that I was squeezing past them, that our bodies were so wonderfully close. Everyone here was as free as I felt, and I laughed, the sound lost to the endless *thumpa-thumpa-thumpa* and the stomping of feet. Glassy-eyed and slurring, people pawed at one another like animals. Their smells were flustering; scents that were usually kept secret flooded the air like a gas.

And yet . . . none of it was quite right.

I emerged from the crushing sea of people by the bar. Fauxhawk caught sight of me as I appeared, then smiled and waved me over.

He said something as I came close, but even with night-time hearing I couldn't make it out.

"What?" I shouted near his ear.

"Hey there!" he shouted back over the music.

"Hey. Blaze, right?"

"Miss Webb?"

I nodded, then grabbed his hands. "Want to get tangled up in me?" I purred.

He laughed. "What if I burn you up?"

"You're corny!" I shouted.

"So are you!" He winked. "But it's all good. I like that."

I pulled him off his stool by his hands and started to lead him toward the dance floor, but the keys were cutting into my palm. I should have brought a handbag.

Holding up my pointer finger to Fauxhawk, I shouted over at the bartender, "Hey, you got any string or anything?"

He leaned close. "What drink?" he shouted.

"String!" I shouted back. I held up the keys. "I want to hang this from my neck."

Nodding to show he understood, he grabbed a box from beneath the bar. Bottles rattled inside, and it was held closed by twine. Using a pocketknife, he snipped free the twine and handed it over.

"Thanks, man. You rock!" I shouted at him.

He smiled blankly at me, then gestured to his ears to show he hadn't heard.

"Thanks. You—!" I shouted louder, then turned away. "Forget it."

Quickly stringing the key ring on the twine, I tied the makeshift necklace round my neck and tucked the keys under my dress. Then I grabbed Fauxhawk by the hand and led him to the edge of the dance floor. "Now let's dance!" I shouted at him.

He didn't hear me, but he didn't have to. The song changed to something that sounded remarkably similar to what had been playing when I came in, the lights flashed, the crowd cheered. I spun around and let the thumping beat take over, thrusting my hips and throwing my hands in the air, tossing my hair and sweating horribly, but not caring. Fauxhawk grabbed me by the hand and spun me, then put his hands on my waist and pulled me in close. He ground his body into the back of mine, and I reached my arms back to wrap them around his neck.

Everything about this was something my normal daytime self would never do, even more so than drinking at the party. This was way better than the high school stuff, I decided. People here were looser, less self-conscious. No wonder so many other kids got fake IDs.

I could feel Fauxhawk's heartbeat against my back, could feel the hot lash of his breath against my neck. I was in complete and utter control of him, dominating and muddying his mind more than alcohol ever could. I could sense his rationality fading away as his want for me grew.

He spun me toward him and put his face close to mine. His stale cigarette breath filled my nostrils.

"So, baby, you want to come back with me?" he said

into my ear. "Me and Bobby over there have our own place not too far, we could take the party there."

I laughed. "No, no," I said. "I'm just here to dance." I tried to pull away from his grip, to get back to dancing. He wouldn't let go.

"Come on," he said. "You got me bad, Miss Webb. You got me all wrapped up here, got me squirming."

I sniffed him again. His stench was ordinary, stale, unappealing. Once more the urge to find the one with the right scent flushed over my skin. I'd been close enough to someone so damn perfect that his scent was now permanently etched in my brain. Someone cute but otherwise only serviceable—like this guy—couldn't compare. It was maddening, but it made my answer easy.

"I can't," I shouted into his ear. "You don't smell right."

He started breathing harder, faster, pulling me in close and putting his forehead to mine. "Don't play me, baby. You know what you're doing, but we all hate games. . . ."

God, this guy was repetitive. I dug my fingernails into his chest and shoved. Surprised by the force of my push, he tumbled backward against another dancing couple, then glared at me.

"What the hell!" he bellowed.

"I said *no thanks*." I rolled my shoulders back. "Besides, I'm only sixteen. You'd totally get arrested."

His face went blank. "What?"

"It's true." I turned away, calling back, "I'm getting bored. I'm sure you can find someone else around here who's actually legal."

Leaving Fauxhawk standing there stunned, I shoved through the heaving bodies toward the stairs.

Back up on the top floor, I stretched my arms and legs in the relative roominess. The bass-filled music didn't seem quite as loud anymore and the people here were more subdued, off in their own private worlds.

"You know you're not supposed to be in here."

The voice was right next to my ear. I spun around to find a blond vision behind me—Deputy Jared in a tight red T-shirt. In his hand he clenched a bunch of flyers.

The dancing, the heady sensations, everything here was good—but not as fulfilling as I'd hoped. Something was missing. Maybe Jared could fill that emptiness.

"Well, hey, fancy seeing you here," I said as I moved in close. I grasped him around his waist and pulled our chests together. The echoes of his heartbeat pulsed through my body, almost in time to the beats of the music blaring around us.

He wasn't fazed at all. "Seriously. Emily, right? Aren't you sixteen?"

I sighed and stepped back, almost bumping into a pair of

women walking by. They stumbled but just laughed before wandering off.

"And aren't you off duty?"

He smirked at me. "Right. Well, I don't know how you got in, but now I've got to escort you out. It's my civic duty."

I rolled my eyes and walked past him. "Come on, don't be such a Boy Scout. Why don't you dance with me? It'll be fun, I promise."

He followed as I wound past chairs and other club patrons, then stepped in my way. "You know, Emily, I heard some things about you."

"Oh?" I said. "Awesome things, I hope."

He rolled and unrolled his flyers as he regarded me. "Well, I heard that you are a nice, quiet girl who likes to stay home and watch movies on Friday nights. And yet here you are, out on the town alone, dressed like—" He gestured at me, his flyers flapping. "Well."

Find the one who smells right. Find the others.

The thoughts came unbidden, bombarding my brain, pulsing to the club's beat that endlessly assaulted my ears. Not even Jared could keep away these urges. Especially not if he was going to insist on being so insufferably *good*.

I inhaled, taking in more of the sensual odors surrounding me. My head went woozy.

I needed to find someone else. Immediately.

"Right, well, I can take care of myself. Now, if we're not gonna dance, I'm going to—"

He put a gentle hand on my shoulder. "I get it, Emily, really. I don't want to get you in trouble. I did a lot of stupid things when I was sixteen too. It's just been really hard seeing kids not that much younger than me getting hurt lately. There's a murderer out there, you know."

I arched my brows. "Is that why you made photocopies of the police reports and passed them around like salacious reading material?"

"No, I just thought maybe it'd hammer home how dangerous it can be out there." Trying to guide me forward, he turned so that we were side by side. "Come on, I'll take you to your car and make sure you get home okay."

"Yeah, no, I'm good, but thanks anyway." I freed myself from his gentle grip, bumping him in the process. His stack of flyers—all emblazoned with a Bubonic Teutonics logo—went fluttering to the floor.

He dropped to his knees to pick up the flyers, and I started to walk off to find a non-police-officer guy to have fun with.

And then I smelled it. The musk.

It wasn't quite the same as Patrick's wonderful scent, but it was close enough, like Dalton's had been. Someone was nearby who was like me. Someone male, someone who smelled different from everyone else in the club.

It was like I'd been dying for a drink and someone just walked by with a pitcher of water.

I'd resisted the urge all evening, but I couldn't do it any longer. I didn't know exactly what I was going to do with him when I caught him. But it didn't matter—every part of my brain was screaming at me, demanding I seek out the source of the scent.

Sniffing at the air, I made my way past the couches to the spiraling staircase that led to the roof deck. Behind me I heard Jared calling my name, but he couldn't see where I'd gone, so I ignored him. Up on the roof I found that the couples had left, replaced by three guys laughing with one another while talking about things I didn't particularly care about. Ignoring them as they catcalled at me, I strolled to the edge of the building, nostrils flared, following the scent trail.

Down. He was down there, in the alley. And close, too—his smell even overpowered that of the rotting garbage in the Dumpster.

I vaulted over the side of the building, not worrying about using the ladder. I landed on the fire escape below with a loud, metallic ring. Then I half ran, half leaped down the stairs to the bottom fire escape, put both hands on the edge, and flung myself over.

I landed in a crouch in the alley. The aroma was strong

now, so wonderfully strong, but I couldn't see him. Still sniffing, I marched forward, past the Dumpster.

It was as though I was standing right on top of him. My fingernails dug into my thighs in anxious anticipation—this wasn't the right one, but perhaps he was one of the "fellows" I'd felt compelled to seek out. Oh, but he would do. We could dance all night, and Fauxhawk and Jared and everyone else would just fade away.

He wasn't there. He had to be there. *Needed* to be there.

But I couldn't see him, even as his musk swirled around me, slid into my nostrils, dug into my brain, drove me to keep searching.

My heel stepped on something hard, and glass crunched. I crouched down and discovered a broken vial lying there, thick, clear liquid in a puddle around it. A biohazard label was affixed to the part of the vial that wasn't shattered. I sniffed again. The smell was incredibly strong, making me light-headed, like I'd just drowned myself in a vat of perfume.

The smell was coming from the puddle. From the broken vial.

"What the—"

There was a shuffling behind me. Immediately I stood up and spun around. A dark, shadowy figure stood there. He was tall and slender, a long overcoat hanging to his knees, a wide-brimmed fedora hiding his features.

"Emily Webb?" the figure asked, his voice deep and gravelly, almost as though he was disguising the way he really sounded. "Daughter of Caroline and Gregory Webb?"

"What?" I asked again. "How did you—"

I couldn't finish as his odor hit me. The man's stench was overwhelming; he smelled like a laundry pile that had spent the summer fermenting in the boys' locker room. I gagged, even as I realized that this smell had a feeling. It felt like . . . fear? No. Nervousness?

"Yes," the man grunted, his tone flat and emotionless. "You're her."

The man raised his arm and pointed his finger at me. No, it wasn't a finger jutting out of the man's dark sleeves. It was the barrel of a gun.

A gun.

My heart thudded, and a flurry of thoughts flooded my mind in the moment before the man pulled the trigger: *Leap at him, duck, scream for Jared, runrunrun.* The thoughts were a din of incomprehensible noise, and I froze, my legs heavy and dead and unable to take me away.

I began to open my mouth to speak, to say something to make the man stop whatever it was he was going to do. Instead I felt my lips curl into a snarl, baring my teeth.

And the man pulled the trigger.

13

NOT NOW

Flame flared from the gun's muzzle, flashing like the strobes inside the club. The flashes were followed by two small, almost unimportant pops.

And though my mind was frozen, turned to mush by fear at the sight of the gun, some unknown instinct screamed *Move!* in my brain, and I flung myself to the side.

I swear I felt the breeze of the bullets fly past my head like a pair of flies buzzing close to my cheek. Somewhere down the alley, the two bullets hit a wall with two little clinks.

I rolled, and found myself crouching beside the stained Dumpster. My chest heaved, my heart burned with anger—he'd tried to shoot me. Someone was trying to kill me!

Steady, clicking footsteps as the man walked purposefully around the Dumpster to finish what he'd started. *No,* my mind raged. *You will not hurt me. You will not hurt me!*

I grabbed the edge of the Dumpster. Something damp oozed between my fingers, but I didn't care. Tensing my arm muscles and with a primal scream, I shoved. The Dumpster creaked in protest, then spun away from the wall.

The man yelped. Another flash as the Dumpster careened into him, another pop as a bullet fired uselessly into the air. The Dumpster banged against the brick wall on the opposite side of the alley.

I couldn't see the man, didn't know how much damage I'd done. But I could hear him breathing, could hear the rapid beating of his heart, smell his rancid stench.

Again anger flared within me. Clenching my fists, I tramped forward, ready to pummel him for what he'd tried to do to me, for what he'd done to Dalton, to Emily C. And then I would carry his limp body inside, drop him at Jared's feet, and show that know-it-all deputy that I really *do* know how to handle my business.

I cried out as stars burst behind my eyes. My stomach heaved, my arm hairs prickled. Doubling over, I clutched my gut.

"No," I sputtered. "Not now!"

I could hear him moving. He'd fallen, had been knocked

over and momentarily stunned by the twirling Dumpster. I could end him. I took another step forward, then dry heaved.

I had no choice. Reaching out blindly toward the damp brick wall beside me, one hand grabbing my stomach, I turned and careened down the alley away from the man, forcing my feet to move even as my head howled, demanding I lie down in the trash, let the pain overtake me, let the change come that I now knew had never been a hallucination.

I staggered out from the alley, into the street. Horns beeped at me, people walking down the street stared, bright lights flashed, and tires screeched as someone swerved to avoid hitting me. I ignored it all, ran into the next alley and the next, splashing through stagnant puddles and nearly tripping over a homeless man curled under an old army blanket.

The pulsating behind my temple turned into a squeezing sensation, like my brain was swelling, bursting free of my skull. I couldn't keep the change at bay any longer. Finally, in a new alley, behind a new Dumpster, I moaned and fell to my knees.

My hands throbbed like I'd dropped a desk on them, my nails tugging at the skin of my fingers as though trying to pull free. I held my trembling hands to my face, watched as the nails blackened and grew long and sharp, tearing free of my cuticles. My eyes watered as bones crunched and lengthened, the sensation like getting a tooth drilled while jacked up on Novocain. Coarse, dark hair appeared on my palms, spread to my wrists, climbed up my arms.

My arms. They quavered uncontrollably, feeling as though someone was pounding them with rubber mallets. Like with my hands, it hurt only distantly, but it was horrifying to see my skin twisting as my bones *moved*—malleable, rubbery things that stretched and stretched, pulling tendons to their limits, forcing my muscles to grow taut, hard. The same thing was happening in my legs, and I could feel my now-clawed toes slice through Dawn's black shoes, my heel elongating, forcing the heels off with sharp *pop*s.

My gut and my chest seemed to bubble beneath my dress, contorting and twisting, the sensation stinging like I was in the midst of doing a dozen crunches. The dress. Stupid as it was to think about something like that in the midst of transforming into a frickin' werewolf, I didn't want to ruin Dawn's dress. So I fumbled and shrugged the dress over my head, balling up the shimmering fabric and letting it fall to the ground.

I grabbed at my chest—it had flattened and grown hard, muscular. My stomach narrowed into tight knots, and fur spread here, too, covering me in black and gray. I wanted to scream at the absolute wrongness of it all, fall to the cobbled stone of the dirty alley and cry, but something new was taking over. The part of my brain that had been whispering its strange urges to me for days now was pushing me back, asserting itself over Daytime and Nighttime Emily both. It was calm and focused, forcing me to relax and let the changes finish.

There was a tugging at the base of my spine, a sharp pain at my tailbone, and something pushing its way into my underwear. For a moment I thought I'd messed myself, but no, no—I knew what it was. Modesty completely out the window, I sliced with my claws, my underwear falling to the ground in tatters. A long tail unfurled and slapped at the back of my legs.

Finally the pressure in my brain burst, my skull becoming puzzle pieces rearranged by unseen hands, pulling and stretching to make my mouth and nose into a snout, to drag my now pointed ears to stand at attention atop my head, to file my teeth into sharp, saliva-dripping fangs.

And then, finally, it was done.

I had changed. I was no longer Emily Webb, Daytime or Nighttime.

I was the wolf.

Whatever was left of my normal brain was too stunned, too freaked out about someone trying to kill me and the realization that werewolves were real, to do anything. The instinctual wolf brain wanted to take over completely, and I let it.

Something dangled around my neck. I pawed at it with my claws: Megan's car keys. Some part of me recognized I needed to keep those close, remembered the muddied dress lying at my feet. Because even though I was mostly wolf now, I was somehow still Emily, still me, still all the parts of me.

I snatched up the dress in my jaws, sniffed at the night air. Discarded fish guts in the Dumpster near me. Diesel exhaust from the roads. Brine on the breeze coming in from Puget Sound.

But I didn't smell the killer's horrific stench. Didn't smell the false musk he'd used to lure me out of the club.

He was gone. But for how long?

The moon was a razor's-edge sliver in the sky above me, its now gray glow searing my pupils. I turned back the way I'd run, the wolf brain knowing without ever being taught that sticking to the shadows was safer.

That man had tried to murder me. I needed to protect myself. Protect my unknown mate.

My mate? The Emily side of me, still mostly overwhelmed, laughed bitterly in my brain. That was what all this was about, wasn't it? The urges to smell guys, the frantic search for the right one. The wolf side of me wanted to mate.

No matter. To the task at hand.

I stalked forward. My claws clinked against the concrete; I breathed in short bursts through my nostrils. The shooter had been two or three blocks north of where I was. He couldn't have gotten too far. I would—

I stopped. I wasn't alone. Someone, something, was watching me within the alley.

I turned to the Dumpster, once green but now dark gray to my new eyes. There, beside it, stood a shadow. Just a shadow, nothing more, in the shape of a man but cast by no person that I could see.

Whatever I had been feeling, been sensing, was there whenever I changed. Wherever I went. It was completely still, featureless. There was a depth to the shadow's blackness, a solidness even though my human brain knew, rationally, something like that could never be solid.

But the wolf side of me knew for certain: The shadow watched me. It could see me.

Some ancient, primordial fear edged into my head. The longer I stood there staring at the unmoving shadowman, the more my heart pounded, the more my strong limbs trembled.

I couldn't take it anymore. Letting out a muffled whine,

I spun away, southward, away from the direction of the club where the killer had found me. I dropped to all fours and bounded out of the alley, fleeing the watching shadow with its unseen eyes.

I stuck to the backs of buildings until I was forced to run out into the open. It was late, cars were fewer, people were less present, though not gone entirely—not in a big city that's awake at all hours. I took chances and darted across roads and through an empty sculpture park, until I reached the parking lots opposite the docks with their storefronts and restaurants opened up onto the water, boats bobbing on gentle waves. Keeping low, I darted between cars parked underneath the viaduct above my head, hiding in its shadows as I headed south.

My paws hurt as they slapped against the rough concrete and asphalt. The wolf me hated the city. Hated the endless stone, the lack of trees, the absence of others like me to run with. My frightened wolf brain and my frightened human brain agreed on one major point: I needed to get home.

I ended up in the shipyards, winding between metal cargo containers stacked atop one another like a giant's multicolored Legos. Steel cranes towered high above, like the remnants of long dead dinosaurs, gray bones that still supported long necks that stretched over the dark water of Puget Sound.

I don't know how long I ran; it must have been hours.

But with the wolf's singular focus, the distance didn't matter, nor did the time. I bounded over wire fences, slunk behind houses, crawled through underbrush, still hearing the endless sounds of civilization—parties behind closed doors, planes flying overhead, cars zooming down the highway.

And finally, finally, I was back to familiar ground. To the suburban streets of my neighborhood. Where before the wolf had decided that even here was too artificial, now the lawns and trees were a comfort after the long night of racing through a city of steel and concrete.

I found myself in the woods near my house. The perfect woods, where pillars of tree trunks rose to hold up the sky, nocturnal creatures darted through branches to avoid me, damp leaves cushioned my claws instead of rubble digging into the soft pads of my transformed hands and feet.

I had trouble breathing; the wolf brain longed to drop the stained dress still held tight in my teeth. It was bad enough having the jingling keys smacking against my chest as I ran, the twine digging into the fur around my neck.

But I refused to drop the dress. Not after I'd already destroyed so many of Dawn's clothes; this one needed saving. Instead, I snorted for air through my nostrils as, finally home, I came to a stop in the trees.

I smelled him then.

My mate.

My human side was terrified by what this meant—it could be the killer trying to trick me again. Waiting behind the trees with another vial of liquid musk open at his feet, waiting to shoot me.

The wolf side, the dominant side, didn't care. My head snapped to attention. I strained to be sure. Some part of me just knew: This wasn't like Dalton's smell, and it also wasn't like the scent that had wafted off the puddle released by the killer's vial. This was the real thing.

My nose told me all: My mate was here. After my long, thrilling, and terrifying night, how I needed him. I had searched for him for far too long already. I had to know that he was all right, hold him close to me and nuzzle his neck.

With renewed focus, I darted through the trees, kicking up leaves and dirt as I ran. I sniffed the ground, ignoring other animal smells, following his.

And then there he was.

He was far away, deeper in the park and moving steadily. Thanks to the pale streetlights that managed to glow through the canopy, I could see clearly that my nose had been right: He wasn't a normal wolf. He was like me—half human, half wolf; tall and gangly, humanlike muscles covered with dark fur, his face elongated into some bastardized version of a real wolf's head.

I wanted him to smell me, to turn and run to me. But he kept moving. I could howl to catch his attention, but then I would drop the dress, and still my human brain refused to do so. So I followed, not worrying about being stealthy, bounding through the underbrush like a noisy, bulky, careless human.

He broke through the last line of trees before I did, loping out onto a suburban street toward a row of small houses. I didn't see which one he ran toward as I, too, reached the street, but the part of me that was still Emily Webb recognized where I was from my years driving through my small hometown.

I longed to follow the scent to my mate's comforting side. But exhaustion washed over me and I found I could no longer run. My head felt light, woozy. Heart thudding against my transformed chest and my insides tightening, I knew my night was coming to an end. I had to get somewhere safe. Had to hide from eyes that would see me transform back to normal.

The run home was a blur, but soon I was standing outside the two-story home I'd known for years. Even though it was so terribly human, it smelled comforting to my lupine nostrils. This was where I belonged. Where I would be safe from men with guns, from men of shadow.

I wanted to leap up and through my bedroom window, but after the long run home from Seattle, I could no longer perform such feats. Instead, eyes drooping, I staggered into the backyard. There, in the back corner, was our old toolshed. Standing on my hind legs, I pulled the door open with my claws, then crawled inside.

No longer able to keep my eyes open, I collapsed to the rough wood floor, a rake and the lawn mower shadows above me. Spitting out the soggy, messy dress, I panted, my tongue lolling free from between my sharp teeth.

So tired that I felt it to my bones, I rested my wolfish head atop my long arms, and I slept.

Partial Transcript of the Interrogation of
Branch B's Vesper 1
Part 4—Recorded Oct. 31, 2010

F. Savage (FS): So he had some sort of bottled pheromone he used to lure his victims. That would be one way to do it. But how he found you when—

Vesper 1 (V1): When you couldn't do it? Maybe he just had better tipsters than you did.

FS: Emily, you understand that we tracked you and your fellow deviants down not to harm you. You were simply, ah, mistakes that needed to be contained until we could help you return to a normal life.

V1: So now I'm a mistake?

FS: No, it's not . . . Look, Emily, all I am saying is that our sources were not looking to bring you any harm.

V1: I know your sources, Mr. Savage. And I guarantee you that's exactly what they wanted.

[Silence.]

FS: I can sense you're feeling overwhelmed when it

comes to the subject of the killer—
V1: I'm not overwhelmed.
FS: —and so we can move on to other, more important
subjects detailed in this past chapter.
V1: Like the shadowman?
FS: Er, yes, though I am sure you are aware they
are actually—
V1: If you can call me a deviant, then I can call
them shadowmen.
FS: Fair enough. Then let us talk about your im-
pressions of—
[Loud thumping sounds, most likely from outside the
room. Muffled shouting can be heard, also from out-
side the room.]
FS: Oh my.
V1: Okay, something is seriously going on out
there.
FS: I—I will be right back. Stay here.
[Chains clang.]
V1: I'm not going anywhere.
[The door to the room can be heard to open and
shut. The muffled thumping and shouting continues.]
V1: So I guess it's just me and me.
[Moment of silence, save for sounds outside the
room.]
V1: Sounds like Mr. Savage and his friends have
their hands full. Good.
[Silence.]
V1: I'm thinking of smashing this tape recorder. I
am saying this out loud, because I'm going to re-
sist that urge. I want you to know I thought about
it but didn't do it. Instead I'm going to leave

this recording intact, and I'm going to leave behind everything I wrote. So you won't forget. So
you—
[The door to the room can be heard to open and
close once more. Outside noises have ceased.]
V1: What was that all about?
FS: Ah, yes, yes, it was nothing to concern yourself with. Just a slight situation. But we have it
under control.
V1: You do? That's a relief. Sounded dangerous.
FS: Nothing to worry about. I, we, have nothing to
worry about. We'll get back to the subject of the
shadowmen later. For now, let's continue. It's getting late.

14

WHEN WILL IT BE ME?

Gray, misty daylight slowly filtered through my eyelids. Groaning, I clenched my eyes tighter, mumbled something about needing five more minutes, and tried to roll over to get away from the morning sun.

Splinters scraped against my bare back and I yelped. I sat straight up, rubbing at my back and feeling little shards of wood stuck in my skin.

And I realized I was sitting in the middle of our tiny, dusty toolshed, completely naked.

Realizing something like that? Yeah, it'll wake you up right quick.

The night came back to me in a rush—drugging Megan, stealing her car, teasing an older guy at a club, being a total jerk to Jared, getting shot at, turning . . .

Turning into a wolf.

Trembling from shock, and from the cold air seeping through the cracked-open door, I hugged myself, covering my bare chest. The car keys still dangled around my neck, the metal cold against my skin.

Part of me didn't want to move. Wanted to stay inside the toolshed, surrounded by yard tools that looked all blurry to me without my glasses—the lawnmower with bits of ground-up grass stuck to its side, the rake and the pruning shears, the nail gun and the saw hanging from the back wall. If anything, I was safest in here. Lots of weapons if the man from the night before came back, pulled his gun on me, tried to shoot me . . .

And I wouldn't have to go outside, face the day as rational, emotional Daytime Emily, the only one of my apparent three personalities that ever had to frickin' deal with the actions of the other two.

But I was so cold, damp from early morning dew, and my back stung from where I'd lain against the plywood floor. I felt around until I found Dawn's sparkly blue dress.

I held it up and grimaced. Sequins had fallen free and it was wrinkled, stained with mud, and stiff with dried wolf-girl drool. Part of me wanted to cry. I'd tried so hard to keep the dress Nighttime Emily had stolen from Dawn safe. Lot of good that had done. But another part of me felt . . . pride, I suppose. Because I'd changed into something monstrous, but I'd still kept part of me there. Kept in enough control to at least have some priorities. Which I couldn't say about myself when I was Nighttime Emily.

The ruined dress was disgusting, but it was all I had. I pulled it on, feeling like I might as well have put on nothing but a potato sack for how exposed I still felt without any underwear on. Reaching out an unsteady hand, I grabbed the top of the lawn mower and pulled myself to my feet.

The door to the shed opened with a creak, and I blinked, trying to get used to the daylight. Everything was blurry—if there was one thing I could actually keep from my transformation into Nighttime Emily, I wished it were her perfect vision.

Grimacing as I stepped onto sharp, wet blades of grass, I quietly made my way to the back door. I had no idea what time it was, but I could tell it was early. Maybe no one was up yet, no one had realized I was even gone. As willing as my dad was to let me more or less off the hook for my party shenanigans, I knew that even our Daddy/Leelee bond wouldn't keep him from completely exploding upon discovering that I'd done it again.

The back door was locked, and I realized that I'd stupidly only grabbed Megan's keys the night before. I hadn't even bothered to take my own house keys with me. Certain that I'd have to ring the doorbell to get inside and give myself up, I walked around the side of the house to the front door. Taking in a breath, I turned the knob.

It was unlocked.

Exhaling slowly through my nose, I quietly opened the front door and crept inside the foyer. Shutting the door as silently as I could, I tiptoed toward the stairs.

That was when someone coughed.

Stiffening, I slowly turned to face the dining room table. Megan sat there in the same clothes I'd left her in the night before, half-moon shadows under her pale eyes as though she'd been up all night.

Her lip trembled and her nostrils flared at the sight of me. I didn't know what to say.

"Hi," I whispered.

She shook her head slowly, her face flushing red. "You did something to me," she finally managed to bark out. "You stole my frickin' car, Emily. And all you say is 'Hi'?"

Fingers fidgeting with the hem of my dress, I looked askance toward the stairs.

"Please," I whispered. "I can explain everything. Just . . . did you tell them? When everyone came home last night, did you tell them I'd left?"

Megan slapped her palms against the dining table. A

little bowl of apples in the center bounced up and clattered back down.

"I didn't need to tell them anything," she snapped. "You had it all planned out. They probably saw my car was gone, assumed I had left, peeked in your room and saw someone they thought was you sleeping under the covers, then went to bed themselves. Pretty smart, Emily."

Standing up, she sent her chair screeching back against the bare wood floor. I gritted my teeth. She was being way too loud.

Megan held out her hand. "Can I have my keys?" she said. "I've been up since three thirty waiting for you, since my brother called me, telling me that Jared told him you were out on the town, and that he wanted to make sure you got home okay. Sounds like you had a fun time out."

Fighting my trembling hands, I dug the keys out from under my dress and lifted the makeshift twine necklace over my head. Megan's eyes darted up and down as I dropped the keys in her palm, taking in my state of disrepair for the first time. For a moment, concern flashed over her face.

"Your dress," she said. "And you're barefoot. . . . What happened?"

I opened my mouth to answer, and she waved her hand. "Never mind," she said. "I don't care what you were doing with your new little popular friends, I don't want to hear about it. Just tell me where my car is parked. I'm leaving."

My jaw hung slack as I struggled to find some way to explain. Giving up, I sighed and said, "Seattle."

"Excuse me?" Megan narrowed her eyes and leaned across the table. "Did you just say *Seattle*?"

"Yeah, uh . . . ," I stammered. "I sorta kinda left your car parked next to a club in Seattle near the Art Institute. A place called Frenzy."

"You left—," she sputtered. "You took my car to Seattle? Why would you leave it there? How did you even get home?"

I crept around the table, hands raised. "Shh, shh," I said. "Please, please don't wake them up, okay? A lot happened to me, and I can explain everything. Let's just go upstairs, all right? We can take a cab to Seattle, get your car, maybe talk on the way."

Megan's face was red again, her jaw taut. She didn't say anything, so I backed away, then turned to head up the stairs to my room. She followed.

Safe in my room with Megan, I shut the door and let out a long breath. Megan went to sit on my bed, the covers a mess.

I didn't know where to start. So, tugging at the bottom of my dress to make sure my privates were covered, I ran around the room gathering clothes and my glasses, then opened up a little green case I'd stuck next to my computer, inside of which sat several twenty-dollar bills. I had been saving up to buy my dad the complete *Buffy the Vampire Slayer* series set on DVD for Christmas. Regretfully, I plucked four of the twenties from the pile. Clutching the clothes I had gathered to my chest, I handed the money to Megan.

"So we can get to Seattle by cab," I explained meekly. "And pay whatever I owe for where I parked the car."

Megan snatched the money from my hands. She refused to say anything.

"Well," I said. "Um, I'm going to go take a shower really quick, and then I'll tell you what happened, okay? I didn't know that I'd lie to you about when I changed last night, I promise. It wasn't me who put the sleeping pills in your drink, it was Nighttime Emily, I swear."

Megan's mouth snapped open in shock. "So you *did* do something to me? You drugged me with frickin' *sleeping pills*?"

"No, not me," I stammered. "It was Nighttime Emily, it wasn't—"

She waved her hand dismissively. "Whatever. Go take your shower."

"Can you call Jared and tell him I'm all right?"

Megan turned away from me, disgusted. "Fine."

I watched as Megan took out her cell, and then I walked slowly across the hall to the bathroom. Setting my clean clothes and glasses on the counter, I bent over the tub and cranked the "Hot" knob all the way, steam curling up to fill the bathroom and fog the mirror.

I lifted the destroyed dress off and let it fall to the floor. My body aching, I climbed into the shower, shut the plastic curtain. Hot water sliced into me like heated needles, turning my skin pink. I closed my eyes and scrubbed myself with my loofah, washing away the filth of the night, cleaning the splinters from my back, scrubbing the grass stains from my feet.

And then, letting out a gasping sob, I sat down in the tub and clutched my knees.

I struggled to breathe as tears burned at my eyes. Everything in my life had changed so rapidly, and I didn't know how to handle any of it. A week ago I had been the same person I'd been all my life—quiet, reserved, geeky little Emily who spent her days dreaming about being like the other teenagers and having the confidence to do more with my high school years than stay shut up in my room all the time.

Be careful what you wish for, right?

Sitting there with the harsh water pounding against my face, I felt afraid for the first time. Nighttime Emily's antics were often way out of line, but whatever worry I had about that change was always tempered by a giant dose of excitement—of enjoyment at my new confidence, my new ability to kick butt and take names.

And maybe I hadn't even been afraid about turning into a werewolf—a frickin' werewolf. There was something about the werewolf thing that made my head reel with wonder, because it still didn't feel *real*. It felt more like another fantasy made reality—turning into something better and stronger than myself.

My main memory of my time as the wolf the night before was, with the exception of the shadowy figures I'd seen, a sense of fearlessness unlike anything I'd ever felt before, even as Nighttime Emily. To be able to let the wolf side of me take the driver's seat? That was actually sort of . . . neat. And so my stupid geeky side actually sat there and thought, *Cool!* even as my rational side realized that my life had just become a lot more complicated.

No, what had me shivering with fear was the man in the alley. The dark figure with the gun and the gravelly voice, luring me, targeting *me*. Just like he'd snuck up on Emily C. and Dalton. I'd felt bullets fly by my face, narrowly missing me, and though Nighttime Emily had only felt pissed off, now that I was me again, I felt way too mortal. I couldn't die. I just couldn't.

It was only then, sitting in the shower, the little textured fish cutouts rough against my skin, that I realized I wasn't anonymous anymore. Not just for getting crazy at a party, or for dancing wildly at a club. Someone out there, someone I didn't know, wanted me dead. He didn't care that I wanted to grow up, figure out who I was meant to be.

Someone wanted to take that from me, and even though Nighttime Emily could throw Dumpsters, and Werewolf Emily had terrifying teeth and claws, most of the time I was Daytime Emily and I would be helpless. It wasn't an idle *What if it was me?* any longer. It was a dreadful, crushing *When will it be me?* I could go outside and he could be there, as shadowy as the ghostly figures I'd seen when I was the wolf. He'd raise his gun, pull the trigger . . .

I couldn't think about Nighttime Emily just then. Couldn't think about whether I was going crazy or still hallucinating or if I was actually a monster. I had no one to talk to about those things, and thinking about them now, with the threat of that man with the gun still out there, would drive me insane.

But I could talk about the shooter.

Maybe not with my parents or the police or even Deputy Jared, not without them discovering my secret lives, realizing I was some freak of nature and turning me over to scientists to slice me open and discover what I was. But I could talk with Megan. I could always talk with Megan.

She couldn't understand the change into Nighttime Emily, and I wouldn't dare tell her about the werewolf change, but this . . . maybe she could help me.

Grabbing the edge of the tub, I pulled myself to my feet. I wiped my eyes, then rinsed my face in the water before turning the shower off. Toweling myself dry and putting on my hoodie and glasses, I snagged the dirty dress from the floor and tiptoed across the hall back to my room.

Megan was gone.

I snuck downstairs as quietly as I could, discovered the remnants of our milkshake movie evening in the living room—the open *Scream* DVD case, Megan's empty glass with melted ice cream congealed around its base—but did not find Megan. She'd left and was probably halfway to Seattle to go collect her car by herself.

I sat down on the edge of the couch and buried my head in my hands. On top of everything else, I'd alienated Megan, maybe for good.

I was on my own.

I ended up falling into a restless sleep in my room for a few hours before waking up and having the whole night wash over me all over again. But this time, it didn't seem quite as bad. It's amazing what your mind can rationalize before it snaps for good.

Still, I couldn't help but feel like I would look out my window and see the shooter, his rimmed hat shadowing his face as he leveled a pistol at me, prepared to snuff me out forever.

I hid in my room for half the day, not even going downstairs to eat despite my aching stomach. My dad came to check on me after a while and I lied, telling him I just had a lot of schoolwork that I wanted to get done, convincing him to give me back the cord to connect my computer to the internet so I could do research.

I gathered all the books I'd checked out of the library and spread them around me on my bed. Clutching Ein in my lap, I skimmed through them, trying to find variations on the theme that would explain what was happening to me. But the legends were all the same—a werewolf bites a person, person then transforms into wolf at the full moon, yadda yadda. Nothing about the transformation beginning with a crazy mood swing, or turning into a wolf when the moon was at half-mast or nonexistent, or turning without even being bit by a hamster, let alone a wolf-man.

Frustrated, I tossed the books aside and instead dug through my DVD case. I had a number of werewolf movies: *Dog Soldiers*, *An American Werewolf in London*, *Teen Wolf*, all three *Ginger Snaps*, *Cursed*. With the exception of

Teen Wolf, the stories were pretty much the same—man (or woman) turns beastly, massacres frightened humans, has to be put down.

Reassuring.

Okay, so DVDs weren't really going to help me out all that much either. I could find similarities in books, in movies, but nothing felt *right*, and once again I found myself feeling alone. I didn't feel hopeless because of this, not really. I was just frustrated. It was bad enough to have originally been the geek who liked things no one at my school had ever heard of, and that I'd alienated half the school by acting like a stripper on crack at Mikey Harris's party. Now I had *this* to deal with.

Every teenager changes when she grows up. Develops new senses and new emotions, grows hair in new places. But not quite like this.

Tossing the DVDs to the floor, I slumped onto my bed and lay back, arms spread wide. The ceiling above me was bumpy and white, though I could make out little yellow spots where once glowing neon stars had been stuck with Sticky Tack.

And then I realized: I wasn't alone, was I? The night before, what I now knew were the wolf's instincts had whispered to nighttime me that I needed to find my "fellows." Others like me? Perhaps I'd been right yesterday when

Megan told me about how Emily C. was killed and how Dalton was shot. Both of them had gone through changes, like me, and now all three of us had faced off with the killer. That wasn't a coincidence.

And I couldn't forget—there was Patrick. Mysterious, brooding Patrick, who had smelled so *right*, had smelled remarkably like the other werewolf I'd seen last night. . . .

There was something happening. Something going on here that I didn't quite understand, but that meant I wasn't alone after all. At least, not before the killer found the mysterious male werewolf I'd seen running through the woods last night. Not before he finished off Dalton and found me again.

I fired up my computer and began doing searches for "Emily Cooke," "Emily Webb," and "Dalton McKinney." I only found a few results for all of our names together, and those were just pages listing all the juniors at Carver High. Yeah, thanks, Google, I already knew we went to the same school.

I deleted my name from the search and tried again. A few more links popped up, all about various clubs and organizations the two had been in.

There had to be something here I was missing.

I thought back to what the man had said to me last night before raising the gun.

Emily Webb? Daughter of Caroline and Gregory Webb?

My parents. That was strange. He'd mentioned my parents. Maybe . . .

I didn't know Emily C.'s or Dalton's parents' names, so I just typed in "Cooke" and "McKinney" and "Skopamish, WA." Shaking my leg, I clicked Search.

Results popped up.

The first: a link to the employee page of a company called BioZenith. For some reason my heart pounded as I followed the link. Under "Notable Employees" I found two familiar names: Harrison McKinney and Marshall Cooke. Relatives of Dalton McKinney and Emily Cooke, perhaps?

There was something here. This couldn't be a coincidence. But the website didn't give much more information beyond the company's accomplishments, using scientific terms that I didn't understand.

I clicked through to the main page of the website, read their little blurb. BioZenith was some sort of bioengineering laboratory dedicated to improving the science of agriculture. You know, making grapes seedless and all corn yellow, things like that. Unfortunately, there wasn't any line on the page that said, "And oh yes, we have some werewolves on staff. Ask us how to join our howlingly fun team!"

So there it was, a connection: two men I was sure were related to Dalton and Emily C. had once worked together, or at least for the same company. The only problem: That connection didn't include me. My dad was a construction worker, my stepmom was a librarian, and before my mom had died she'd worked for Microsoft in their publicity department.

So maybe the connection between Emily C. and Dalton was a coincidence. Maybe there was something else I was missing, unless I'd been kidnapped by crazed corn-altering scientists and that somehow made me a werewolf, made me someone who needed to be killed.

My stomach growled, and I realized I'd grown massively hungry. I also realized it had grown dark outside.

It was almost eight o'clock.

My body seized with fear. I couldn't go through it again, the change into Nighttime Emily, into the . . . the wolf. Not with that man out there waiting for me, wanting me dead. I knew if I didn't do something fast, Nighttime Emily wouldn't be nearly as cautious as I was. She'd probably do a smash-and-grab at a pawn shop, steal a pair of brass knuckles, and go hunting for the guy who'd tried to shoot me.

And she'd end up getting herself—getting *me*—killed in the process.

Was this my life now? Would I have to spend every day filled with dread, knowing that when night came I'd turn into some version of myself I couldn't really control? How could I live like that? How could anyone?

I closed my eyes and took a deep breath, struggling to think, trying to focus on *today* because thinking further ahead than that would drive me crazy. I needed to figure out a way to keep myself from going crazy for the fifth night in a row.

If I was right about Dalton and Emily C. being like me, that they were also werewolves and that was why the killer went after them, then wouldn't it have been all over the news when Dalton had spontaneously transformed into a wolf-man in his hospital bed the past two nights?

The difference between me and Dalton? He had been unconscious both nights I'd turned into a werewolf. Which meant maybe, if I could get unconscious as well . . .

I ran into the bathroom and dug through the medicine cabinet. Finding my stepmother's sleeping pills, I once again snapped open the lid and stole two. Gulping at water from the faucet, I swallowed them down, only then considering that maybe there was another reason I'd turned into a wolf and Dalton didn't.

But it was too late now. The pills were already in my empty gut, dissolving and swirling into my bloodstream, making me drowsy.

Back in my bedroom, I changed into my pajamas,

flicked off the light, and lay down in bed. The last thing I saw before I fell asleep were the glowing numbers on the clock reading 8:04, and the last thing I thought was, *Please let me be right. . . .*

15

COMMUNIST HERRINGS, HUH?

I snapped awake the next morning with a sharp intake of breath, adrenaline surging through my veins, certain that the shooter would be standing over me, gun pointing at my head, preparing to blow my brains out.

I was, of course, alone. I was still in my pajamas, I wasn't covered in mud or drool or scratches. For the first morning in several days, there was no sign that I'd run wild outside.

The pills had worked.

I got up from bed, almost stepping on the pile of DVDs and books I'd unceremoniously tossed to the floor last night. Talk about personal changes—movies and books are sacred to me, seriously. I'm the type of person who files my movies and books by title and/or author and keeps them in the most pristine of conditions. I even keep a little log of everything I own on my computer, from *Books: Adams, Douglas* all the way to *Movies: Zodiac*.

Totally anal, I know. But I've always liked lists, even before my dad got married to Katherine the librarian, a lady with a serious crush on organization.

For the first time in a week I felt rested, my head clear. What had caused overwhelming confusion the day before now seemed . . . almost normal already. Turning into a liberated party girl? Old hat. Werewolf? Who hasn't changed into a mythical beast at least once? I could think about these things as though I was thinking about someone else entirely—as though I was watching a movie where some doppelgänger actress was the one teasing older men and running through the woods sniffing for her mate.

But I couldn't feel that way about the shooter. I was slightly less paranoid than the day before, but he was still out there, still waiting . . .

I got on my computer and did another search: "Emily Cooke." Maybe there had been a break in her murder case, a new article detailing some previously unreleased evidence found on the scene. Something that would connect her back to me. Or maybe I'd get lucky, find out they'd caught the shooter and had him behind bars.

The only new article I found was an obituary. It said

little more than who Emily C. was survived by and that she would be missed. And also that her funeral was to be held that day at noon.

I looked at the clock. It was a little after eight thirty.

I sat there, thinking about Emily Cooke. Here is the sum total of what I knew about her life before she died: She was pretty. Her parents were wealthy. A lot of people liked her. And she and I shared the same first name.

That was a pitifully small amount to know about someone.

It was strange, but I suddenly felt a deep, hollow loss. Nothing had changed about our nonrelationship in the past week, with the exception of the day I had feared she was hovering around me, waiting to possess me. But now I knew that even though it wasn't what I'd originally imagined, there actually *was* some connection between us that went deeper than our names. Something it seemed only a handful of people had shared. And now I'd never get to talk to her about it.

Maybe I was being presumptuous, I don't know. Or just being overemotional because it felt like the only people who cared about me all hated me at the moment due to the way I'd been acting. But if I was right, if the reason Emily C., Dalton, and I had been targeted was something unique to us, something that caused us to change as night

fell, our bodies to transform as we ran under the stars . . .
then I'd missed out. I'd spent so much time being ignored by
the other kids at school that I forgot that I was sorta kinda
ignoring them, too.

It was too late to get to know Emily C., to talk girl to
girl about our shared, monstrous secret. But I could at least
pay my last respects.

After lunch, Dawn drove me to the church where Emily's
funeral was being held. She wasn't exactly keen to go, but
when I told her that I was going anyway, even if I had to
walk there, she insisted on driving me.

I was dressed in black slacks and a black blouse that billowed in unfortunate places—an outfit borrowed from my
stepmom's closet. I peered out the window of Dawn's car as
she pulled into the church's parking lot. It was a clear, bright
day. Next to the church was a park. It wasn't a seesaw-and-
slide park, just a nice, open field with evergreens and birches
swaying in the cool breeze, flowers still in bloom around a
latticed gazebo.

The park usually hosted weddings, but I could see figures dressed in black sitting inside the gazebo, crying on one
another's shoulders. I guessed that Emily C.'s casket would
be moved to a cemetery somewhere else after the ceremony.

The church lot was so full of cars that Dawn had to

park along the sidewalk out front. We filed through the square doors into the chapel, all the pews already filled with somber mourners. I saw teachers from school, including Ms. Nguyen, sitting side by side with friends of Emily's, like Mikey Harris and Mai Sato. Mai cried openly, tears streaming down her cheeks. I don't think I'd ever seen her cry, not even when she'd broken her leg the year before during a track meet.

At the very front of the chapel, set atop a draped table beneath a modern stained-glass window, was a closed coffin. Emily C.'s coffin. Next to the coffin there was an easel set up with a blown-up black-and-white photo of Emily Cooke. It was artistic and incredibly well composed (says me, the girl who digs movie cinematography): She sat on a porch step, pensively considering a lake. Half her face was cast in shadow, as though the picture had been taken as the sun set, and she had a little half smile on her face, like she'd posed super serious but had started to crack up just as the camera snapped.

Looking around at everyone sitting in the pews, I felt completely and totally out of place. I didn't recognize a lot of the people there, but the people I did recognize—mostly the teenagers—had really known Emily Cooke. It was like I was invading another private party of theirs, and for a moment my heart fluttered, afraid that someone would turn around and see me, think I was going to ruin Emily C.'s funeral like I had Mikey Harris's party.

Ducking my head, I grabbed Dawn's hand and led her to stand against the back wall. It was crowded enough that there were a few other people standing as well, so it didn't seem that odd.

The service began with a pastor talking about ashes to ashes, dust to dust—the sort of thing you hear on TV funerals. Guess those are true to life, after all.

The sermon done, Emily Cooke's friends and family stood up in front and talked about her life. Mikey Harris, wearing an ill-fitting suit and with his hair slicked down, nervously fiddled with note cards as he talked about how Emily Cooke was always trying to take everyone's photo, that she dreamed of going professional. He revealed that the photo on the easel was actually one she'd taken with a timer—a self-portrait. So those photos I'd seen on her web page *were* ones she'd taken. She'd been talented.

Mai went up next, tears making little rivers down her cheeks. She recalled how after she broke her leg Emily Cooke would write her long emails every single day, making up short stories about Mai gaining a bionic leg and beating everyone's butt when she got back on the track, or just fabricating intricately long jokes with stupid punch lines to make her smile.

More family and friends stood and shared stories, talked about trips they'd taken with Emily Cooke, about how funny she was, how creative. She wasn't perfect by any means, her father was quick to point out—she was always so busy thinking of things she *wanted* to do, that Emily often forgot all about the things she was *supposed* to do, like the time she offered to give her little sister a perm, then went off to take photos, leaving her sister in the chair, a garbage bag over her clothes and chemicals in her hair. That year, Emily Cooke's sister had to sport a really short haircut.

I laughed along with everyone else at that story, and I realized something: Megan was wrong about Emily Cooke. And I'd been wrong too, thinking she was just about style with no substance. Emily Cooke wasn't just some insipid rich girl. It was funny—I'd spent so long hiding from people like Emily Cooke that I never knew that she and I might actually have some things in common. That we could have been friends.

I also felt sorta guilty, you know? Here I was, meek little me, with no real goals beyond staying alive long enough to see the next *Batman* movie. The other Emily had real dreams, real talent. All taken away by two little bullets put into her by a man whose image was now burned into my brain.

I couldn't laugh or feel sad anymore, share in the stories

everyone was telling. Standing in the church, behind rows of pews filled with black-clad mourners, I began to tremble with anger. It wasn't right, not what happened to me, not what happened to Dalton, especially not what had happened to Emily Cooke.

That man, that *killer*, had to be stopped.

As Emily Cooke's uncle took the podium and launched into a story, the glass door leading outside creaked open. I caught sight of new guy Patrick leaving the funeral early. I hadn't even noticed him, I was so caught up in hearing about the death and life of Emily Cooke.

He always seemed to be around at the wakes for Emily Cooke, despite being the new guy who shouldn't have known or cared about her. And I was sure that he was the wolf I'd seen the other night, the one I was certain was my mate.

I'd had so many opportunities to talk to him, find out what was going on. And I always lost my nerve.

"What would Nighttime Emily do?" I whispered to myself.

Dawn leaned over to me and said, "What was that?"

"Nothing. Hey, I need to go talk with someone."

Before Dawn could protest, I speed-walked to the exit and followed after Patrick. He walked down the street at a rapid pace, cars zooming by on the busy road in front of the church. Shoving my hands in the pockets of my too-big slacks, I followed.

"Hey!" Dawn called as the glass church doors slapped shut behind me. I peered back over my shoulder and saw her winding around parked cars, her expression stern, the way it had been in the car when she'd dropped me off at school Friday morning.

Catching up to me, she grabbed my arm. "Look, dude, no more running off."

"Sorry," I said, "it's just, there's this guy, and I really need to talk with him. And I'm gonna lose him. . . ."

Dawn let me go, crossed her arms, and arched an eyebrow. "A guy, hmm? Is this what all your antics have been about?"

I almost laughed, remembering the wolf-me's thoughts— *Find the mate.* Maybe it *was* all about a boy after all.

"Yeah," I said quickly. "I've gone all chick flick lately, I guess. But we have to hurry, I don't want to lose him."

Rolling her eyes, Dawn actually smiled at me for the first time in days. "All right, girl, let's go get him."

Half walking and half running, so that I looked like the geriatric speed walkers you see at the mall on Sunday mornings, I chased after Patrick, Dawn at my heels. He was at the end of the street now, entering a small convenience store on the corner, the kind that has had the same faded cigarette ads in its windows for decades and where the little wrapped sandwiches you can buy are all queasily green.

Timidly I opened the door to the store and peeked in. It was empty save for the wrinkly Asian woman behind the counter reading a copy of *Entertainment Weekly*, and for Patrick, who stood in the center of the snack aisle, his face stoic and unreadable.

"I'll wait out here," Dawn whispered, then patted me on my back.

With a steeling breath, I stepped inside. The glass door shut behind me, a little dangling bell ringing out. I cringed, but neither the clerk nor Patrick bothered to see who'd come in.

Trying to be nonchalant, I strolled down the aisles. I might as well have started whistling, I was so conspicuous. I dared a glance over at Patrick as I walked past a shelf stacked with little rolls of toilet paper, cheap razors hanging above them on hooks. He seemed to be having a dilemma choosing between a Butterfinger and a Snickers.

This is so not what Nighttime Emily would do, I thought.

I pulled my hands from my pockets, rounded the shelves, and came to stand directly next to Patrick. I couldn't breathe.

"Hi," I squeaked.

Blinking, he looked up, a brief expression of confusion

crossing his face before it reverted to his default of stoic and broody.

"Hello," he said, eyeing me.

There was a lilt to his tone. I'd been right, he had a definite accent. Which was way attractive. Wetness seeped over my palm and my heart pounded, and I was suddenly very conscious of the fact that I was wearing a mourning outfit borrowed from an extremely nonfashionable forty-three-year-old woman.

"So . . . ," I said, kicking at the scuffed tile with my shoes, my arms pressed tightly against my sides, my fingers drumming against my thighs. "You were at the funeral too, huh?"

He shrugged, then went back to rifling through candy bars. "Yeah."

My heartbeat seemed to rush into my ears, like there were drums pounding away next to my head. I was hyper-aware that attractiveness-wise, Patrick was in a totally different league than me. I wanted to duck down and run out of the store, but I knew if I did I'd never figure anything out, so I forced myself to continue.

"You're new, though?" I asked. "I mean, I know you're new, it's just I saw you at the wake-slash-party thing at Mikey Harris's house and now at the funeral. You couldn't have known Emily Cooke, unless you knew her before you went to school with us, or . . ." I stopped and gulped in a breath. "Yeah."

Cocking an eyebrow, Patrick asked, "Do I know you?"

"No!" I said. "No, not really, I just saw you around, thought I'd say hi." I stuck out my arm, my hand stiff. "I'm Emily. Uh, another Emily—Emily Webb."

He regarded my sweaty hand, making no move to take it. "Patrick," he said.

With a nervous smile, I lowered my hand and tried to casually dry it off on my slacks. This was so not going well. I longed for Nighttime Emily's instincts to kick in and take over. If this guy was supposed to be my mate, *shouldn't* she emerge and woo him? That would be so much easier.

Wait. The musky odor . . . I didn't smell anything. Patrick didn't smell.

As smoothly as I could—which was about as smooth as a jug full of gravel and broken glass—I stepped in closer, nostrils flaring as I took in a big sniff. Maybe I just wasn't as sensitive to his scent as Nighttime Emily, and that was why I didn't pick up the alluring musk. . . . Though that hadn't seemed to matter in the cafeteria the first day I'd seen him.

"Uh . . . ," he said, taking a step back from me. "Do you want something? I want to buy a lolly and go, so if you don't want anything . . ."

Nervous giggling erupted in my throat. Gesturing at the shirt he wore beneath his black leather jacket, I said, "Communist Herrings, huh?"

His shirt was red, with a little black fish wearing a tall furry hat beneath the band name.

"Yeah, back in London, little band my mates formed," he said. "Nothing big."

"Oh," I said. "That's cool."

He stared at me. I in turn stared at his shirt and wondered if maybe I could feign stumbling against him, get in a good whiff. Maybe there was something I could say to keep him from leaving until I could be sure he wasn't who I thought he was.

"So . . . you're from London?" I rambled. "That's really cool, I love British people. *Doctor Who* is awesome. I've seen, like, the whole series. Oh, and *Spaced*, too, and *Skins* is just the best thing ever and . . . Um, do you live on Orchard Road?"

The street name from where I'd seen the other werewolf run Friday night popped into my head, and I said it before I could really think about how amazingly creepy it must be to have some strange girl come up to you, act all fidgety, try to smell you, ask a bunch of prying questions, and then name the street on which you lived.

Patrick's eyes darted between the front doors and me like he wanted nothing more than to flee the store. I laughed a little too loudly as heat flushed my skin, and I saw the lady behind the counter lower her magazine and give me the stink eye.

"I'm not a crazy stalker or anything, I promise," I stammered. "Just, I've lived in Skopamish, like, forever, and I know someone moved out from there, so . . ."

"Yeah," Patrick muttered, his sharp eyebrows furrowed as he took a step back from me. "Orchard Road . . . I need to go, so I will see you at school, then?" He gave me one last wary look, then turned and hustled out of the store.

Well. That went just *swell*.

It wasn't until a few hours later, when I'd had some time to dig into ice cream and beat myself up over being so massively lame, that I realized a couple of things about my little encounter with Patrick.

Thing one: He most definitely did not have the smell. No musk, no pheromones, nothing. I wasn't an expert on scentology or anything, but I was guessing your personal scent wasn't exactly something you could shut off.

Thing two: Patrick was tall, and Patrick had an accent. But . . . What would Patrick look like in a long coat and a brimmed hat? What would he sound like if he lowered his voice and faked an American accent?

I sat at my desk chair, stiff, my hands shaking. Because: *whoa*.

I'd been thinking about this all wrong. Patrick had appeared right after Emily Cooke was killed. Even though he couldn't have known her, I kept seeing him at functions where people mourned her death. And there was that book he was reading in the library, the one about serial killers.

The shooter had lured me from the club using a vial of the same type of scent I had smelled on Dalton. That meant that if he wanted, the shooter could slather that smell on himself like some sort of heavy cologne . . . maybe go to school, see what girls were drawn to him. . . .

Maybe cute new guy Patrick wasn't my "mate" after all. Maybe he was the killer.

I sat at my desk for a long time, watching the screen saver on my monitor. It was there that I made a decision.

Emily Cooke was dead. Dalton McKinney was in the hospital. And someone, maybe Patrick, was after me now. I couldn't do much as Daytime Emily. Not when going up and talking to a very cute boy turned me into a jittery, frantic crazy person.

But Nighttime Emily could possibly do something. And Werewolf Emily most certainly could.

That night, I wasn't going to take the sleeping pills. I was going to let the change happen. And then I would go to

Orchard Road, where Patrick lived, where I'd seen the other werewolf run.

And I was going to find whoever was behind this and stop him before anyone was killed, anyone else's life snuffed out like artistic, scatterbrained, witty Emily Cooke.

16

THE WOLVES MUST DIE

I lay in bed, Ein clutched to my stomach, waiting for night to fall and the change to happen.

I'd decided to make it easy for Nighttime Emily. I'd pulled on a formfitting black turtleneck that Dawn had made me buy when she tried to give me a makeover last year, and a pair of black pajama pants. With dark shoes and a knit cap pulled tight over my head, I was a cat burglar by way of an Angelina Jolie movie.

Now all I had to do was wait.

I almost chickened out several times, wavering between anger-fueled confidence and rational *Do not go after a killer!* thoughts. But I realized I didn't have much of a choice—I couldn't tell anyone of authority about my secrets, couldn't call my one friend to back me up without risking her getting hurt. From the articles I'd read about Emily Cooke and Dalton, the police were baffled by the complete lack of evidence left at the crime scenes. They were no closer to finding the shooter, which meant he had another night to stalk the streets, to find me or the other werewolf, to sneak into Dalton's hospital room. . . .

Darkness settled outside. The houses and trees disappeared into blackness, making the whole world seem a frighteningly empty void.

"So," I said aloud as I waited. "Other Emily. I just wanted to thank you for not actually possessing me. Murdered or no, that wouldn't have been cool."

I was met, of course, with silence. All I could hear was the buzzing of my computer.

But I imagined she was there. Sitting in the corner, dressed fabulously, beaming at me. In my head, she had been bled of color, was just black and white and shades of gray. It was hard for me to picture her in full Technicolor.

"I wish I'd known you," I went on, just to fill the silence in the room, talk over my worried thoughts. "I wish I hadn't been too afraid to talk to you. Because I think we could have been friends, you know? You could have showed me how to not explode into nerves around new people, and I could have showed you a bunch of great movies that would totally make you laugh."

My imagined Emily Cooke crossed her legs and tilted her head, her expression not changing. I tried to imagine her saying something back to me—but, I realized, I didn't actually remember how she used to sound.

I took off my glasses and closed my eyes. Lowering my voice, I whispered, "I'll do this for you, Other Emily. Because you didn't deserve what happened to you. And I'm really sad that you're gone."

I couldn't hold on to the image of my fake Emily Cooke, and she faded away. Sadness lurched through me, heavy in my stomach. Which was strange, because I hadn't even known her.

The sadness gave way to a pulsing, determined anger. I *was* going to find whoever the killer was. And he was going to pay for what he'd done.

The change happened, and for the first time I accepted it without even an ounce of resistance. My stomach cramped, my chest tightened, but it wasn't as bad as before. There was no queasiness, no pain. Just a whirling sensation in my head and a pleasant fluttering in my gut, like the feeling you get after an amusement park ride. The transition was over in just a few seconds.

And I was back.

Strength surged through my muscles. Stretching, I tossed Ein off of me, then leaped to my feet.

I raised my eyebrows at the sight of myself in the mirror. I thought I'd looked good while I was Daytime Emily and I was . . . right. Maybe there was hope for my daytime self's fashion sense after all.

Remembering why I was dressed like the next Bond girl, I grinned dangerously. I had a mission: go find the guy who'd dared to trick me on Friday night, who'd tried to shoot me, and finish the job I started when I threw a Dumpster at his face.

I slid up the window, swung over the sill, and leaped to the grass below. I landed softly, delicately—as fugly as they were, the sneakers I'd picked out for myself earlier were certainly practical. Much easier to land on than heels, at least.

I glanced side to side, making sure I was alone, then ran down the street to my left, toward the woods.

I padded beneath the tall trees, my feet crunching over fallen leaves as I moved nimbly around logs and scrubby bushes. There were dirt trails—that was what the woods were for, anyway, a sort of hiking park—but I didn't bother following them. I felt more at ease in the thick of the woods, liked the challenge of finding places to step without making a sound. Besides, I knew exactly where I was headed, and the dark night and the overgrown underbrush weren't going to keep me from making a beeline there.

I emerged from the trees exactly where I'd tracked the other werewolf the other night—in fact, I could still see the deep indents of our clawed footprints in the dirt of the path. Orchard Road was laid out before me, a row of boxy, semi-run-down, small houses. The two houses straight ahead were where I'd seen the other werewolf vanish.

I crouched down behind some bushes as a car drove by, its headlights flaring up over the trees behind me. Blinking to gain back my night vision, I studied the two houses.

One had a shorn, patchy lawn, and hokey painted wooden signs jutting out from a front garden filled with weeds—you know, little gnomes and the backside of someone in a polka-dot dress made to look like she was gardening. There were a few lights on inside, but I couldn't see anyone.

The other house, the one on the left, was similar—minus the corny signs but plus a brand-new, untouched basketball hoop set up in the driveway. I spotted a pair of trash cans on the side of the house, behind which were broken-down moving boxes.

That was the one.

Making sure no one was out on the street and no other cars were coming, I stalked across the road, my sneakers making almost silent little smacks as I stepped on the asphalt. I went around the side of the house with the basketball hoop, running my hand against the plastic siding as I crept along.

At the back of the house, I found one window lit up, the blinds open just enough so that I could see. Gripping the edge of the windowsill, I peeked in and saw Patrick.

He was wearing a pair of long pajama bottoms and a white T-shirt. For a moment I just watched him through the slatted blinds—he looked incredibly hot with his dirty-socked feet crossed, a pair of oversize headphones on his ears, and his sharp brow furrowed in concentration as he read his book.

Then I saw the title of the book and realized it was the same serial killer one I'd seen him reading the other day at the library. He must have gone back and checked it out.

"Getting tips?" I growled to myself.

His room was bare, except for the bed and a desk. Boxes were stacked in the corner with clothes haphazardly hanging out. Probably not a lot of time to decorate when you spend your evening massacring teenagers.

So what was his deal? I wondered. He was so cute that I didn't particularly want him to be a murderer, but I'd read enough of the R. L. Stine paperbacks my dad kept from when he was a teen to know that you can never trust the cute new guy not to go all wild-eyed and stabby. But me, I was a werewolf, and Patrick, he was from London. Maybe he was from some secret Londonian cult whose sole purpose was to snuff out a werewolf epidemic, like a young priest who needed to rid the world of us devil spawn.

I swallowed a laugh. Certainly my nighttime self was more than a little devilish, but the thing the movies and books had gotten wrong about werewolves: I wasn't some vicious, uncontrollable monster. I was *something* all right, but as I had run through the Seattle night with Dawn's dress clutched in my jaws, I knew I most certainly was *not* a crazed beast. Part of me had still been in there. If I hadn't been so afraid, I could have been far more in charge of the situation, I was certain.

Letting go of the sill, I crouched down and put my back against the siding beneath Patrick's window. I could hear the faint beats of the music he was listening to way too loudly on his headphones, the creaking of his bed as he moved his long, restless legs. Maybe this was how he psyched himself up, listening to death metal while reading about serial killers. Whatever the case, when he left the house, I would be ready for him.

A door slammed to my right, and I heard someone gasping, gagging as he lurched into the backyard of the house next door. Still keeping an ear toward Patrick's window, I got down on my hands and knees and crept forward. I could barely see from the pale light of the quarter moon, but someone stumbled across the patio, clutching at his stomach as he bumped into lawn chairs.

And I smelled it. Smelled *him*.

The other werewolf.

What a coincidence, right? A werewolf living right next door to a werewolf hunter. But if that was the case, why hadn't Patrick taken out the guy next door first?

I decided to make sure Patrick was still where I left him, then go finally grab the other werewolf and find out who it was.

And he was there, right behind me. The shooter.

I froze. He was dressed the same—long overcoat, brimmed hat. But in the light that beamed from Patrick's window I could see his face.

He was old—at least midforties. His face was slender and long, his stubbled jowls slightly droopy. His dark eyes were manic behind a pair of round spectacles that flashed white, reflecting the light.

I had no idea who he was.

"Emily Webb?" he asked, his deep, raspy smoker's voice echoing in my head and bringing back terrified memories of our first encounter.

Without another word, he raised a gun, his finger on the trigger.

I didn't stop to think. I couldn't. Rage coursed through me. Before he could pull the trigger, I snarled and barreled forward, tackling him.

We fell to the grass in a heap, his hideous stink invading my nostrils. I grappled with his flailing arm as he struggled to toss me off, to lower the gun and shoot me. Gripping his torso with my thighs, I grabbed at his gun hand. He kept punching at my side, so I clenched my right hand into a fist and backhanded him.

The force of my blow was hard, harder than I'd expected it to be. He stopped struggling, stunned. I smacked his left hand against the ground so hard that he let go of the gun. It skittered across the grass, disappearing into the darkness of Patrick's backyard.

"So you thought you could screw with me, did you?" I screamed in his face, spittle flying from my lips and speckling his glasses. "You messed with the wrong girl."

Leaning back, I hefted my right arm and punched him in his pasty face. His head snapped to the side, and he let out a startled cry.

"Why?" I shouted. "Why did you kill her? Why are you after me?"

He glared up at me with black, furious eyes. "You . . . ," he snarled.

Grabbing his neck with my left hand, my nails digging into his soft flesh, I drew back my right fist. "Speak up, I can't hear you."

He heaved for breath as I prepared to smack him once more. So much anger surged through my limbs that I thought I could sit there, beating his face in until he was nothing but an unconscious pulp.

And it wasn't just Nighttime Emily there in that moment. Daytime Emily—*me*—was there as well, just like with the wolf, feeling all the anger. And I wanted to feel it. I'd been made a stranger to myself, been put through a schizophrenic hell, and now this man wanted to kill me just like he'd killed Emily Cooke, just like he'd almost killed Dalton.

"The wolves," he sputtered, blood flowing over his thin lips. He wasn't talking in an American accent anymore. His voice was guttural and distinctly European. German?

"What about us?" I asked. "Spit it out!"

"The wolves must die," he growled. "You must not be allowed to find them. . . ."

"Who?" When I got no answer, I grabbed his shoulders, hefted him up, then smacked him back down against the ground.

"*Who* aren't we supposed to find?" I screamed into his ear. I half expected Patrick to come to the window with all the screaming I was doing. Guess his music was up really loud.

Then a sharp, searing pain in my left leg. In his hand, the same hand I'd let go to grab his shoulders, the killer held a heavy, serrated hunter's knife.

With a husky cry, he slashed at my chest. I jumped back as his blade sliced in front of my gut, almost splitting me open. Floundering, I slipped on the grass and fell on my butt.

He was on his feet so quickly I almost didn't have time to react. He leaped at me, knife flashing as I crawled backward, my heels kicking up grass. With a grunt, he stabbed down with the knife, and I rolled out of the way. The knife sliced into the earth with a soft *thunk*.

I shouted and lashed out with my leg, my sneaker catching him in his ribs. He sprawled left, hand flailing wildly to grab the side of the house.

I jumped to my feet, half crouched and arms spread wide like a linebacker. The killer's eyes darted frantically over me, as though unsure what to make of it when one of his victims actually put up a fight. Then he matched my position, standing across from me in the house's shadows. We circled each other warily, tensed and waiting for the other to make a move. He twirled the knife in his fingers.

My lips curled into a smile, and the killer's brow furrowed with confusion.

"Oh the tables, how they've turned," I said.

Behind him, the other werewolf tilted back his long head and howled up at the night sky.

The killer froze, then very slowly turned around. The werewolf, the one I'd heard stumble from the house next door and whose smell was so overwhelmingly attractive, stood on his hind legs, dwarfing the shooter. The wolf snarled, baring long, skin-shredding teeth, and his yellow eyes flashed dangerously in the light from Patrick's bedroom window.

I could still hear the loud music leaking from Patrick's headphones. I almost laughed—a battle was raging outside his room and he hadn't a clue.

For a long moment, we all stood still, tensed and waiting. A panicked sweat wafted off the killer in waves, and his knife hand trembled.

Then the killer half shouted, half screamed, and slashed at the wolf with his knife. The other werewolf dodged the blade easily, growled, and swatted the killer across the face with his sharp claws.

The killer ducked, his free hand clutching at his bleeding face as he ran into the neighboring backyard. He slipped on the grass, but managed to right himself as he reached the other house's patio.

The other werewolf bounded after him. I heard a loud *clang* and a *thump* as patio furniture was tossed aside; heard the killer's angry cries, the wolf's deadly growling.

I stood where I was, my chest heaving, my vision red

with anger. My fingernails and toenails ached, my stomach and chest squirmed beneath my turtleneck. Like Daytime Emily awaiting her transformation into me, I welcomed the transition to Werewolf Emily with open arms. I was strong, but the wolf was stronger. And right then, all I cared about was getting the man who'd killed Emily Cooke, put Dalton McKinney in the hospital, and tried to kill me not once, but twice.

It hurt. I didn't care. My face was molded into a new shape as though I was made of clay. A tail sprouted from the base of my back and slipped through the hole I'd cut in my pants. The sneakers I was wearing tore into leathery shreds as my feet grew, but the turtleneck and pajama pants stretched along with my mutating body. I was certainly the most fashionably dressed werewolf in town.

And then it was done. My vision had gone gray and my brain was overwhelmed with smells: the wet grass, the metallic scent of freshly drawn blood, my mate's musk.

A terrified, pained howl sliced into the night, and my pointed ears perked to attention. My mate—he was hurt. The killer had hurt him!

Snarling, I got on all fours and darted into Patrick's backyard. I saw them there, the werewolf and the killer, facing off on the patio. Wicker chairs lay on their sides, used charcoal from a fallen grill was scattered over the concrete.

The other werewolf stood there, clutching at his gut, dark blood oozing between his claws. He whimpered, then snapped his jaws at the killer as the man looked for another in with his knife.

I crept forward behind the man, my sharp nails clicking against the patio floor. He whirled and faced me.

Surprise, I wanted to say. But all that came out was a snarling yowl.

The other werewolf's eyes narrowed with resolve. As though we'd been hunting together all our lives, we both lowered our bodies and circled the killer. We took long, sidling steps, growling from deep within our throats.

The killer made a break for it. He dashed between me and the other werewolf, running for all he was worth through the yellowed grass of the backyard.

Not fast enough.

With a howl, I bunched my legs and leaped. I soared through the air before landing right at the killer's heels. Then I opened my jaws wide and grabbed his right arm between my teeth. He screamed as I dug my clawed feet into the grass and pulled back. His hand loosened, and the bloodstained hunting knife fell to my feet.

Struggling out of his long overcoat, he continued running, but the other werewolf was in front of him, and the man had nowhere to go.

The wedge moon lit his face up to my wolfish eyes as though he was standing in broad daylight. This droopy old man had tried to kill me. Tried to kill Dalton and the other werewolf. Had succeeded in killing Emily Cooke.

Emily Cooke.

One of my pack, I realized.

The thought came from my wolf brain, and though I wasn't quite sure what it meant, it felt right. This man had stolen from me one of my own, and fury sizzled through my veins, pounded in my head. My human brain shut off, Daytime and Nighttime both, so enraged that I couldn't handle the way it made me feel.

But the wolf brain knew how to handle it just fine.

In unison, the other werewolf and I growled. Saliva dripped from our fangs. We closed in on him on all fours—one step, two. The mania was gone from the man's eyes, replaced with fear.

Snarling, we leaped.

We crashed into a heap with the man beneath us. Both of us went for his throat.

I don't know which one of us got there first; it was all a blur of bloodlust and the killer's high-pitched, terrified shrieks. My teeth tore into some part of him and I wrenched my head from side to side. The man's screams turned to gurgling gasps, and at last, he fell silent.

Chests heaving, we backed away from the man's still form.

His throat was gone, completely torn free to leave a gaping, jagged wound. Blood was pooling under his head and staining his dark shirt. Which one of us had gone for the throat? The human part of my brain didn't want to know.

Rage seeped away and the girl side of me was stunned, ashamed of what we'd done. The wolf was content now, satiated; I let it take over. Its instincts right then were all that would keep me from going insane over the fact that I had just helped kill a man.

The other werewolf limped back toward his house, whimpering plaintively. He walked partially on his hind legs, one clawed hand on the grass while the other clutched at his wounded stomach.

I bounded over to him. He sniffed me, inspected me with dark, sorrowful eyes. I nuzzled his neck with my own, patted his back with my claws.

Shivering, the other wolf fell to his side and curled into a fetal position. Bending down, I nudged away his hand, sniffed at the blood pouring from his chest. I licked the cut, cleaning the wound, soothing it.

And I sensed something. Sensed *them*.

My head darted up from the other werewolf's chest, craning to look back at the man we'd killed. And there, hovering silently around the body, three man-shaped shadows studied the killer's remains with featureless, dark faces.

Terror seized within my chest, and I whimpered. Slowly the shadowmen's heads turned in our direction. They walked across the grass toward us, their legs moving at half speed as though they were trudging through molasses.

As the shadowy figures came close, I realized they weren't solid: I could vaguely see the line of trees through their torsos. My whole body stiffened, the wolf longing to run but knowing that the other werewolf couldn't run with me, not with his injury. And so, even as my furry limbs trembled, I clutched the other werewolf tightly, protectively, and didn't move.

The phantom beings stopped, their heads tilted to the side as they regarded us. After an endlessly long moment, they raised their arms and brought their hands together rapidly.

Though the action produced no noise, I realized: They were *applauding*.

Then they were gone. No *poof*, no fancy CGI dissipation. One moment there, the next, gone.

I had no idea what to make of what I'd just seen, and I was so terribly exhausted. Not wanting to be afraid anymore, I gave in to the one good emotion I felt: the incredible sense of ease that washed over me after having finally found the wolf—the boy—I'd been chasing for so many nights.

I curled up behind the other werewolf and put one long arm over his back to hug his fur-covered chest. He whimpered and I held him close, comforting him as we both fell asleep in the grass, under the stars and the sliver-moon, while just a few feet away the body of the man who'd set out to kill us gazed blankly up at a night sky he could no longer see.

Partial Transcript of the Interrogation of
Branch B's Vesper 1
Part 5—Recorded Oct. 31, 2010

F. Savage (FS): Oh. Well.

Vesper 1 (V1): You look queasy, Mr. Savage.

FS: Yes, that was all a bit . . . graphic. I don't do well with blood, I'm afraid.

V1: I don't either. Well, at least I didn't used to.

FS: I suppose now is a good time to discuss the, ah, "shadowmen."

V1: If you want.

FS: As you were the first of the deviant subtypes to be able to see the shadowmen, please explain how you felt.

V1: I only ever saw them as wolf-me. And I thought I made it pretty clear how I felt when I saw them.

FS: You were frightened, yes, but could you sense anything more? Did your, ah, wolf-self sense a purpose in perceiving the shadowmen?

V1: No.

FS: No?

V1: Nope. I pretty much felt afraid and wanted them to go away.

FS: There were no other . . . emotions? No hope? Or elation? Nothing of that sort?

[Silence. V1 doesn't respond.]

FS: Ah, well, as you did not encounter the shadow-men again during this first week, I suppose we can touch upon this subject when we discuss the future accounts you shall write.

V1: I guess we can.

FS: For now, let us compare our respective discoveries on the killer, one Doctor—

[A beeping noise sounds.]

V1: You have a text.

FS: I heard, thank you.

[Silence.]

V1: What's it say?

FS: Hmm? Oh, nothing, it's nothing.

V1: Is it about those noises we heard earlier?

FS: It's none of your concern. Let's cut this particular conversation short. I think, since we keep getting interrupted, we should focus on finishing your account. And then I shall resume your questioning at a more opportune time.

V1: Fine.

17

BUT FIRST, SOME CLOTHES

I awoke the next morning so early that the sun barely peeked over the trees. Sensations overwhelmed me.

My arm cradled soft skin. My clothes were damp with dew. My mouth tasted rancid, a rotten film coating my teeth and throat.

I blinked my eyes open and found that my face was buried in messy brown hair. The back of someone's head.

No, not just someone. The other werewolf. The guy I'd been chasing and who I'd thought was Patrick, but who most certainly could not have been.

I sniffed at the boy's bare neck to be sure. The smell wasn't as strong as when I was Nighttime Emily or Werewolf Emily, but it was there. A soothing, comforting, musky cologne that made me shiver inside. For a moment I lay there on the yellowed grass, my arm over his chest as it rose and fell with his sleeping breaths. Low, steady heartbeats thumped beneath my hand.

And then I realized: Though I was still dressed in my pajama pants and the tight black turtleneck, I was lying in some stranger's backyard, spooning a naked boy while—

The killer.

I stiffened and sat up, letting go of the boy and looking behind us. Without my glasses, everything was blurry. But I could see enough to know that the body was where we'd left it, lying so very still. A crow sat atop its chest, bobbing its head down to investigate the dead man's open neck.

My stomach roiling with nausea, I picked up a small rock and tossed it at the bird. It cawed, flapped its wings, and flew into the gray sky.

I closed my eyes and turned away. I didn't want to see the body. Couldn't think about what had happened last night, even though part of me was glad for it. I suddenly realized why my mouth tasted so horrible, and I wanted to be sick.

The sleeping boy who was also a werewolf moaned and started to rise. I opened my eyes and looked down at his pale, bare stomach where he'd been cut. But the wound had healed, leaving nothing but a faint scar. And I realized that my own knife wound—the one on my leg—was gone as well. My eyes traveled up to the boy's chest before going back down to his waist.

I stopped myself and immediately snapped my eyes back up to his face, my cheeks burning. Rubbing at his eyes with his hand, the boy blinked up at me.

It was Spencer. Short, goofy, nice-guy Spencer.

His thick eyebrows scrunched with confusion. Then, smiling, he said, "Hi, Em Dub."

"Hi," I whispered.

The past week came back to me, and I felt so stupid for not putting it together sooner. When I'd first smelled the other werewolf in the cafeteria, Spencer had been there, handing me an invitation. He was there at Mikey Harris's party, too, the smell disappearing with him when he left to go chase after Dalton and Nikki—two people he'd never caught up with. Because like me, he'd changed the night of the party. He'd run into the woods, and my drunken, wolf-ish self had chased after him.

I had spent so much time focusing on the cute new guy I hadn't even stopped to consider that maybe the smell wasn't coming from him after all. Patrick had never been the one; that's why he hadn't smelled like the wolf-me's mate in the convenience store. Not because he was the killer.

Spencer gazed around the yard, his eyes settling on the killer's body. His face fell, and some part of me wished that he would look away from the terrifying mess we'd made, smile at me again. He had a cute smile, I thought. A nice, broad smile that made his face light up, made him seem friendly and innocent.

"He's dead," Spencer said flatly.

"Yeah. We . . . we killed him last night. We . . ." I let out a gulping sob and had to bite my lip. It hit me just then, all of a sudden, what had happened.

I was a monster, after all. A vicious creature, just like the movies and the books told me I was.

"Hey," Spencer said, his voice low. He sat up and brushed a finger under my eye, wiping away the hot tear that had started to fall down my cheek. "No, don't cry. We had to, you know? He was coming after us. We had to keep each other safe."

Swallowing back the tears, I met his kind brown eyes. He smiled again; not the broad, energetic smile, but a small, reassuring smile. My insides fluttered, and I found myself reaching out to grab his hand. I never in a million years thought I'd be brave enough to do that, be so near a boy as regular old Emily Webb without transforming into a jittery motormouth. But being around Spencer felt *right*.

Like we were meant to be together.

And he had said "us." I wasn't alone. Even though Emily Cooke was gone forever and Dalton would be in the hospital for who knew how long, I had found another person like me, someone who knew exactly what the past week of my life had been like. Someone I could talk to about everything without having to keep any secrets.

"Spencer," I said. "How long . . . did you know about me? Do you know why we're like this?"

He shook his head, his longish bangs falling into his eyes. "I don't know," he said. "I was sort of hoping after I saw you change last night that you'd have all the answers."

I laughed despite myself. "Yeah, I know the feeling. There's so much I want to talk about. All of this, it's like we're in a movie or something. I totally expect soft music to play right now as we go to the closing credits."

"Yeah," he said. He stood up, put his hands on his bare hips. "We need to figure out what to do with him. Maybe . . ."

His eyes went wide and he glanced down. Immediately his hands shot down to cover his exposed crotch and he spun away from me. I caught a glimpse of a little more than I should have, half of me feeling completely mortified and the other half wanting to laugh uproariously at the awkwardness of it all.

"Uh, but first, some clothes." He ran off toward his back door, disappearing inside and leaving me sitting on the grass.

I saw the killer's black trench coat lying in a heap on the grass. The right arm was torn to shreds and stained with blood.

Standing, I walked over, wet grass squelching between my toes. I picked the coat up, wrinkling my nose at the stink that rose from it, then dug through the inside pockets.

My hand hit something smooth and cool. I lifted out a leather wallet and dropped the coat at my feet.

There was little inside the wallet: a few dollars, a scrap of paper with some names written down that I didn't recognize. Also in the wallet was a worker's badge from the same local bioengineering firm that had come up when I Googled Emily Cooke and Dalton McKinney: BioZenith.

"Agriculture, huh?" I muttered.

The badge was fuzzy to my lens-less eyes, so I squinted and held it up close. It had the dead man's picture on it, though in the photo he was slightly younger and not quite as pale, his cheeks shaved smooth. Beneath the picture was the name "Dr. Gunther Elliott."

And then the pieces came together, because though I'd had the answer for *what* had been happening to me, I still didn't have the answer to how or why. Now the connection between the other Emily, Dalton, and the killer was clear: a company devoted to biological engineering. A place that, even though it seemed completely outside the realm

of possibility, could perhaps biologically engineer . . .
werewolves.

Someone had done this to us. Many someones. I still
didn't know the why, but I knew the how. This place, this
BioZenith, had done something to us. When or for what
purpose, who knew? Because they apparently never bothered to, y'know, tell us what was going to happen. They
changed us, and they set us loose, and then sent one of their
employees to come kill us.

I glared down at Dr. Elliott's ID, my hand trembling, my
jaw clenched. I felt it again—the anger of the night before.
The rage I'd felt toward the killer had faded when he died.
But now I knew: There was more going on here than I had
imagined. More people were involved who had messed with
us—with *me*—without even asking.

"What's that?"

I jumped and turned to find Spencer standing there in a
pair of sweatpants and a T-shirt and holding two glasses of
water. He flinched, sending water sloshing over his hands,
and I realized how furious I must have looked.

I breathed out and forced my expression to soften. It
wasn't hard. For some reason, Spencer's presence made a
rush of calm come over me.

Spencer handed me one of the water glasses and
explained, "For your mouth."

I took a sip of the water, swished it in my mouth, then spat into the grass. It helped a little to get rid of the aftertaste, but not nearly enough. I longed for my toothbrush, then remembered Spencer's question.

"It's his ID," I said, holding up the badge. "He worked at a place called BioZenith. I'd never heard of it until a few days ago, but two guys with the last names Cooke and McKinney also worked there. I think . . . I think they may have had something to do with the way we are."

Spencer nodded, his thick brows furrowed. "Yeah, maybe. There's definitely a connection."

Putting the badge back into the wallet and shoving the wallet back into the coat, I asked, "What about you? Anyone you're related to work there?"

"Not that I know of. You?"

I shook my head as I stood back up. "No."

"Weird."

We stood there in silence for a moment, shuffling our feet and sipping our water. I realized as I did that the turtleneck I was wearing was far more formfitting than anything I'd ever before dared wear outside of my house, by day at least. Part of me, the part of me that hadn't experienced the last week, wanted to blush and cover myself, make myself invisible or something.

But I didn't. I felt . . . comfortable in my own skin, I

guess. For once, I didn't feel so horribly misshapen or embarrassed, at least not with Spencer, the nice, slightly dorky guy who I never before gave a second thought, but who now made me feel more at ease than any other person had since I was a kid.

"So . . . ," I said, breaking the silence. I wanted to broach the subjects of everything that had happened—the werewolf change, BioZenith, the killer, the creepy shadowmen I kept seeing when I was a wolf. But I didn't know where to start, especially not with a dead body so close by. It was all so overwhelming.

Spencer laughed nervously. "Yeah, sorry. I'm not used to this whole killing-in-self-defense thing, got kind of lost in my thoughts." Spencer bit the inside of his cheek, tilted his head at the body. "What should we do with him?" he asked.

Covering up a murder, even in self-defense, wasn't really something I made a pastime, so for a moment I stood there with my mind blank. And then I remembered that I actually, somehow, had recently made the acquaintance of a guy at the local police station.

"I think," I said, "that I can take care of it. Can I use your phone?"

I had to wake Megan's brother up incredibly early in the morning to get Jared's phone number, but luckily Lucas was so groggy that he didn't ask questions. I then made a quick phone call to Jared. All I had to do was say I needed help and he offered to stop by. Stand-up citizen, that guy.

Spencer's house was quiet and empty. I sat in his living room, alone, as I waited for Jared to arrive. Everything in Spencer's house was sort of low-rent and musty, like the beige couch and the shaggy rug and the tan entertainment center had all been bought at a flea market or Value Village or something. Little decorative tea sets were arranged all around the room, chintzy porcelain cups and plates with pictures painted on them that were fuzzy smudges to me without my nighttime vision.

Spencer's mom and dad were gone visiting his older brother at college in another state, which was good for us, I supposed, since explaining the screaming from last night, the dead body, and the need to wash off the dried blood on our faces would have been sort of awkward.

Next door, from Patrick's house, I heard a car door slam and an engine rev. As it did, the back door to Spencer's house creaked open and he hustled inside. He was still in his sweatpants and T-shirt, though he'd now accessorized the ensemble with a plastic grocery bag over his hand.

"Is your cop friend here yet?" He balled up the plastic bag and tossed it in a trash can near the back door, then came and plopped on the couch opposite me.

"Not yet," I said. "Did you . . . you know . . ."

"Yeah, it's all rearranged."

"Wow, rearranging a crime scene," I muttered. "First breaking into nightclubs, now covering up murders. Wonder what's next for crazy Emily Webb."

Spencer gave me an appraising look. "You broke into a nightclub?"

My stomach sank. I suddenly really, really did not want to seem like a wild-child freak to him. But I was saved having to explain by a car pulling into the driveway.

I hopped to my feet and opened the front door as Jared came up the walkway. His blond hair was more tousled than usual and his eyes were heavily lidded, as though I'd woken him up. He offered me a friendly smile anyway as he came to the door.

"So I hear there's trouble," he said as he came to stand in front of me. "With you, I'm hardly surprised."

My face burned. "Well, I . . . uh . . ."

"Hey, man." Spencer edged his way beside me and held out a hand to Jared. Jared, to his credit, did not act horrified that I was basically half-naked with a boy, alone, at six in the morning. He took Spencer's hand and shook it.

"It's out back," Spencer said. "Thanks for coming."

Spencer led the way to the backyard and showed Jared the scene. Jared stopped cold as he saw the body of the killer. While he stared rigid-faced at the gory remains of last night, Spencer and I explained our story: We'd heard a commotion outside the night before, but hadn't seen anything, just heard muffled shouts and dogs barking. This morning we'd woken up and . . . found the body.

Jared didn't say anything for what felt like a million years.

"There have been reports coming in," he said finally. "People seeing wild dogs running through the hiking park. No attacks or anything, but I guess that's changed. What makes you think the victim is Emily Cooke's killer?"

"Well, the weapons, for one," Spencer said.

We crossed the grass to the body, and Spencer showed Jared the dead guy's arsenal. He'd retrieved the gun from Patrick's backyard with the plastic bag, and now both it and the knife were next to the body—the knife rinsed clean of our blood.

"You can go all CSI on the gun, right?" I whispered. "Compare it to the bullets that the guy used on Emily C. and Dalton?"

Jared's eyes scrutinized me. But there was no denying that some sort of animal had taken this guy apart. There was no way he would think I had done it. No way.

"Yes," he said finally. "And if it is him . . . well, I guess karma took care of him, didn't it?" Putting a gentle hand on my shoulder, he turned me away. "I'm sorry you had to see this, Emily."

"Yeah," I said. "Me too."

Jared said he would take it from there and got on his cell phone with his fellow officers, mentioning that though we would have to be questioned, it could be later, after the shock had worn off. My chest felt tight as Spencer and I walked away—lying to the police? Not something I would ever have considered doing.

But I had to. For Emily C. For Dalton. And for Spencer, too—and the others like me. Because with the wolf's instincts telling me to seek out my "fellows," I was betting there were more of us. Those of us who had survived, we were safe now. My *pack*—if that was the word—was safe.

Spencer and I stood on the patio and watched as Jared kneeled down to inspect the killer's trench coat, continuing to talk on his cell phone while reaching in and finding the same wallet I had.

"So," Spencer said. "I guess it's Monday. Strangely, I don't feel so excited to run off to school."

School. How incredibly strange it felt, after a weekend of clubbing and run-ins with a killer, to have to deal with something as utterly mundane as *school*.

I took in a long breath. Spencer smiled at me, and once again I felt my heart flutter. "Do you think we have time to go somewhere before school?" I asked him.

"Like where?"

I glanced back at the body, still lying in the grass with flies buzzing around its neck and chest. "I think we should see if Dalton has woken up," I said. "And I want to see where exactly this BioZenith place is."

18

NICE TO MEET YOU, EMILY WEBB

Spencer let me borrow a pair of shoes that were too big for my feet, then drove me home. I got there before anyone was awake, and I snuck up to my room to find my glasses and some new clothes. A quick Google search brought me once again to the BioZenith web page; I jotted down the address on a piece of notebook paper and shoved it in my pocket.

That done, we took the twenty-minute drive to Seattle and Harborview Medical Center, where Dalton was still recuperating.

There was barely anyone at the hospital that early in the morning, just some employees in scrubs and addled people wandering around. The place smelled clean, antiseptic— the scent brought back memories of being rushed to the emergency room when I'd gotten supremely sick with the flu as a kid, and it was almost as though I could feel the heat in my head and bile in my throat all over again.

I guess the staff had come to expect visiting high schoolers early in the morning, and a nice nurse led us upstairs to Dalton's room. She left Spencer and me there alone.

Dalton lay in a hospital bed, his skin paler than usual, his red hair a matted mess. Tubes ran into his nostrils, his arms. Balloons and cards and flowers littered the countertops and his bedside, and complicated machinery hummed quietly, keeping track of his heartbeat and other important functions.

"I can't believe he survived getting shot in the head," I whispered.

Spencer stepped through the door to stand beside me. "I sort of can. With the things we can do."

Spencer's big eyes were strangely sorrowful beneath his thick eyebrows. We hadn't talked much during the car ride; I guess both of us were lost in our thoughts.

"Have you done crazy things too?" I asked. "I jumped out of a moving car and hung on to a tree once."

"Wow, really?"

I nodded, resisting the urge to grin at the admiration in his voice.

"Nah, I haven't done anything like that," he said,

looking back toward Dalton's still form. "But I feel stronger. I can lift things. I lifted our refrigerator at home just for fun. And I can see things so much better, like things far away. It's . . ."

"Kind of cool?" I whispered, finishing the thought.

He didn't say anything. He didn't need to. It felt completely wrong to be comparing notes about our shared powers, I guess we'd call them, with Dalton lying so close.

Dalton's attractive face seemed off, somehow, like the left side was a bit askew. A thick bandage covered the top of his forehead, behind which I knew a bullet had entered his skull.

I didn't know what I had expected to see, really. Though I could still smell his unmistakable werewolf musk, all I saw now was the same Dalton who'd been going to school with me for years. Ginger-haired, clean-cut, attractive, and seeming as innocent as any boy can be.

"What are *you* doing here?"

The voice was female and undeniably annoyed. Jumping, I turned to the doorway to find Amy Delgado standing there, glaring hatred at me while Nikki Tate stood beside her, pointedly looking away.

I reached down and grabbed Spencer's arm. He didn't seem the least bit fazed.

"Hey, Nikki," he said. "Amy. We were just checking on

Dalton before school. He seems like he's doing better."

"He is," Nikki said. "We got some good news this morning. The police called to tell me they may have found the killer dead. I came to tell Dalton."

"That's wonderful news," Spencer said. "I just wanted to see him. He looks better than I expected."

Amy's lips were pursed as she slowly shook her head, her mane of black hair trembling about her shoulders. "That's great, Spence," she snapped. "But why would you bring *her* here after she—"

Without even thinking about it, I let out a sigh of exasperation so loud that Amy stopped speaking. Instead she gaped at me.

My first instinct was to try and play it off, shrink in on myself, duck my head. But you know what? The night before, I had gone head-to-head with a crazed man intent on killing me, and I may have been the one who killed him instead. I'd just discovered that a bunch of scientists had probably done something to me for some reason I didn't know. At that moment, I was too damn exhausted and angry to care what Amy Delgado or anyone else thought of me.

And so I didn't back down. I rolled back my shoulders and met Amy's withering expression with one of my own. "You know, Amy," I said, "I hadn't been here to see Dalton since the shooting, and I just wanted to see for myself if he was okay. And he's okay. So now we'll go and leave you three alone, all right?" I turned to Nikki. "By the way, I'm really sorry about the party. I wasn't myself, and I've felt really guilty about it."

Nikki shrugged. "All right," she said.

Amy's hands were clenched at her side and she seemed about ready to leap at me and go all catfight. Through clenched teeth she said to Nikki, "'All right'? Really?"

"It's fine, Amy," Nikki said in a soft voice. "They were just leaving. Right?"

"Right," I said.

I pushed sideways past the two girls and into the hallway, my head light and my insides wobbly. Had I really just done that? I realized I had, and I felt completely frightened and, also, totally exhilarated.

Keeping my head up, I walked purposefully past gurneys and down the hall. As I did, I distinctly felt a hand shove me in my back. I stumbled, my sneakers squeaking on the linoleum. I spun around, certain Amy had chased after me and tried to push me down. But she was still all the way back at the entrance to Dalton's hospital room, her arm extended, her palm aimed at me. No one else was anywhere near me.

Amy rotated her hand around and clenched down all her fingers except for the middle one. She flashed me a knowing smirk.

Okay, that was strange. Something was definitely up with her.

Spencer shoved past her and jogged down the hall. "Sorry about them," he said. "Those girls can sometimes be a little, you know, *intense*."

"Yeah," I said as I resumed walking through the brightly lit halls, trying not to bump into nurses and doctors walking the other way. "Just—"

I stopped as I caught a glimpse of a tall, dark-haired figure in the hospital's lobby. Patrick. He had his back turned to us and was on his way out. Why he was there, I didn't know. But part of me wondered if maybe he was there for Dalton too.

Patrick definitely wasn't a werewolf. And he hadn't been the killer. But maybe there was more to him than just a case of mistaken identity.

But I had too much to process right then without wondering what was up with Amy and Patrick. No, I needed to focus, as I had one more place I needed to go before school.

"What is it?" Spencer asked.

"Oh, nothing," I said, and I pushed through the hospital doors and into the parking lot. "Just, after last night,

I really find it hard to worry about what Amy and Nikki think of me."

"Yeah, I hear that."

Spencer opened the passenger-side door to his car, then ran to the opposite side. We got in and he asked me, "Where to now?"

I pulled the crumpled notebook page from my pocket and smoothed it out over my jeans. "Next stop, BioZenith."

The place was pretty easy to find. It was in an industrial park north of Skopamish, and was more or less on the way back home, just a few exits earlier. Though woods surrounded the area to the north and the south, the industrial park was all pavement and giant, boxy buildings interspersed with pristine roads.

We drove down a winding street lined on either side with trees cut to be all trunk and round top, like lollipop topiaries. Beyond the overly manicured trees and the sidewalks, the buildings sat together, shiny cars parked sporadically in front of them. Some of the buildings were all glass, reflecting the bright sun that had burst through the gray clouds sometime that morning. Others were beige brick, with semis parked in loading docks on their sides.

There were concrete square signs aimed at the street, but they didn't have any business names on them, just street numbers. I read the signs as we drove slowly past until I finally saw the one we wanted: number 304. BioZenith.

"There," I said, pointing out Spencer's window.

He pulled over and parked his car along the curb opposite the sign, and we both studied the structures beyond.

BioZenith turned out to be a series of dual-level white brick buildings connected by glass walkways. We were on the northernmost street of the industrial park, so behind the buildings were the peaks of evergreens. The offices on the north side of the building would have a nice view.

There wouldn't have been anything all that noteworthy about the place—except that it was the only business on this street that was surrounded by a tall chain-link fence lined with barbed wire. The only way in was through a pair of gates midway through the south side of the fence. There was no one there, but I could make out a camera atop the fence aimed at the entrance, and there looked to be a call box there as well.

"Is that a laboratory or a prison?" Spencer asked.

I leaned over him and studied the place. "I know, right?" I said. "For a place that claims to only experiment with vegetables, they have a crazy amount of security. I—"

It was only then that I realized I had basically crawled halfway into his lap. Awareness rushed through me, and I scooted back into the passenger seat.

I coughed and tried my best to act smooth. "So, I guess we should . . . regroup? If you're ready, maybe we can talk about what we know. Last night and this morning have been such a rush."

"Yeah," Spencer said. "Yeah, they have." Twisting to face me, he held out a hand. "Well, let's do this properly. Spencer Holt, werewolf and computer geek. Nice to meet you."

"Computer geek, huh? I didn't know that."

I reached for his hand. As our fingers slipped into each other's palms, an electric rush jolted up my arm. Those damn butterflies fluttered into my stomach, and my arms quivered. His smile, his touch—even as they made me go all wobbly, they calmed my brain. I shook his hand.

"Emily Webb," I said. "Also a werewolf, also a geek. But more of an entertainment geek, I guess."

"Nice to meet you, Emily Webb."

"Likewise, Spencer Holt."

We chuckled at our dorkiness, then dropped each other's hands. I didn't want to let go. All I could see were his brown eyes, wide and open and looking into my own. I had never really *seen* Spencer before today.

We held each other's gaze too long, and we both broke off at the same time, clearing our throats.

"So, I guess we should start at the beginning," I said.

"Agreed."

I told my story first. Everything, just as I've recounted it here. The calmness I felt at being with the guy who smelled *right* also made me feel open, able to say anything I wanted without fear of being judged. Because I knew—I just *knew*—that Spencer would understand.

And he did. He listened intently, nodding along, never questioning, never judging me. I finished with the evening before, as I prepared to go after the killer.

"And that's it," I said. "You basically know the rest. I went to Patrick's, and this Gunther Elliott guy found me. Then you came and . . . well."

Spencer let out a low whistle and slumped into his seat. Outside, cars whizzed by as the morning workers started heading to their jobs inside the featureless buildings.

"Wow," he said. "You're brave, you know that?"

I shrugged. "Not really. I didn't really do anything. It was all Nighttime Emily and the werewolf."

Spencer's eyes narrowed in confusion. "But, no, that *is* you, right? Just different parts of you."

That made sense, didn't it? Because maybe the confidence and wild ways of Nighttime Emily had always been a part of me, just something I'd been too afraid to ever let loose. Dawn had always insisted that deep inside me was a great girl waiting to be free, all shiny butterfly emerging from its hoodie cocoon.

It wasn't easy to reconcile the total otherness of Nighttime Emily with what I thought I knew about my everyday self. Not at all. But I kind of liked the idea that Nighttime Emily's ease in dealing with trouble was really some part of me I'd just always been too afraid to tap.

Would I ever manage to figure out how to bring that out during the day? I wondered. Figure out how to shut off the part of me that screamed in fear anytime I tried something new?

My mind raced so much with these thoughts that I almost missed Spencer's story. "I'd be in my room and I'd feel sick and I'd cramp up, like you said you did. But I didn't really go wild or anything. I mostly just got super focused on homework and my computer. . . . I'd been working on building a new computer for the past few months, and I finished putting it together in a few hours. It was like I became some sort of genius."

He shrugged. "I dunno, I guess I was always able to write or program for hours, but I could never really stick to one thing for too long. All my teachers always told me I had a lot of potential, but I was always too lazy to really live up to it."

"So the change made focusing easier?" I asked.

Spencer's cheeks went splotchy red. He was blushing. It was totally cute.

"Man, I must sound like some totally ADD flake with a huge ego." He ran his hand through his already tousled hair, mussing it further. "But yeah, I guess so. It was sort of like there was some block in my brain that wouldn't let me do things to the . . . best of my abilities? And that's when I figured out I might have some other abilities too."

"Like what?" I asked.

"I was kicking around a soccer ball in our backyard," he said, "and my foot went right through it. So, you know, super strength or whatever. I tried it out by lifting the refrigerator next. That was the same night of the party, when I turned into a wolf for the first time."

"That was your first time too, huh?" I asked. "I was, um, kind of out of it. What happened?"

"Well, I chased after you and—"

A car door slammed nearby, interrupting us. We'd been so engrossed with our stories that we hadn't really noticed the parking lots around us getting full, a steady stream of shiny cars zipping down the road beside us. Someone had parked their car in front of Spencer's, and a man in a suit walked by, keys jangling.

I half expected him to knock on the window, ask what we were doing, then call a battalion of armed men out of BioZenith to come drag us away. Instead he walked past and down the street toward one of the glass office buildings.

I craned my head over my shoulder to be sure.

"Weird," Spencer said. I turned back to him and saw that he was surveying BioZenith again.

"What is it?"

"All the other parking lots are filling up," he said. "But no one is going into that bio place."

He was right. Not a single car even approached the gated entrance to BioZenith.

I caught sight of the digital clock in Spencer's dashboard. It read 8:03.

"It's getting late," I said. "We should start heading back to school."

We buckled our seat belts. Spencer turned the ignition and pulled us out onto the street, then headed toward I-5.

"What is it with that place?" I mused aloud. I felt disappointed. I hadn't been sure what I'd see when we went to BioZenith, but I was hoping for something. Some clue as to who was behind this, why we were involved.

"No idea," Spencer said, his eyes on the road. He drove slower than Megan, more cautious. He even kept his hands at ten and two.

So the visits to BioZenith and Dalton's bedside had been more or less a bust. We hadn't learned anything new, really, and I realized that detective work probably took a lot more effort in reality than it ever did in the movies.

But that was okay. Because Spencer being by my side tempered the anger that was driving me to seek out these answers, even after all we'd been through in the past twelve hours. And the more time it took to find out the secrets behind everything, the more time we could spend together.

"Hey," I said as Spencer pulled onto the freeway and sped up. "What were you going to say back there, about the first night we changed?"

He made sure it was safe, then merged. Cars zoomed past.

"Just that I was running out after Dalton and Nikki like Mikey asked me to. Then I smelled you in the woods and I ran after you. I changed into . . . you know . . . and took off running after the smell. But I never caught up with you. I saw those shadow guys, got scared, and went home." He fidgeted with the wheel. "I actually heard the shots, you know. After I changed. But I was so consumed by the wolf that I didn't even do anything to help Dalton. I—I just ran off." His eternal smile faltered, sorrow tightening his features.

"It wasn't your fault," I whispered. Without even thinking, I reached out a hand to touch his arm. "I don't think you could have stopped him. I—Wait. You heard the shots *after* you smelled me and changed?"

He shot me a glance. "Yeah, definitely after. Why?"

I scrunched my face, thinking, because the timeline didn't fit. I tried to work it out while speaking aloud. "It's just that I went after *you*. I wasn't even in the woods when I heard the shots, and I definitely changed after."

"Maybe you remember wrong?" he asked. "No offense, but you did seem kind of wasted."

So he remembered that. Damn.

"Yeah, yeah, I was," I said. "But I remember that part clearly. I didn't change until *after* the shots, and the only reason I went into the woods in the first place was to chase after you."

Spencer popped his right blinker on and merged into the exit lane. "But that would mean that . . ." He turned to me, mouth open in surprise. The car swerved, and he jolted back to attention. Behind us, someone blasted their horn.

"Oh wow," I said as realization hit me too. "There's another one. Another werewolf besides you, me, and Dalton."

"And it's another girl," Spencer revealed. "I felt very, very sure of that."

"A girl . . ."

So there were more of us. At least one other member of our pack who we needed to find. And maybe once we did, she would know more about all of this. Would actually help us finish connecting the dots between BioZenith, the werewolves, the killer, and those creepy shadowmen both Spencer and I had seen when we were the wolves.

At least I hoped so. Because my brain was beginning to overflow with all this new information, and as Spencer rounded a corner and our high school came into view, all I wanted right then was to dive into class work and forget all about this endless, frightening, exciting craziness.

Well, until night fell, anyway.

19

GROWN-UP

The school parking lot was more full than all of last week, and Spencer had some trouble finding a place to pull in. We drove through the student parking lot, gravel crunching under his tires, until we found a spot that overlooked the fenced-in baseball field.

The sky was completely clear now, and the morning sun shone bright over evergreens that rustled in the crisp fall breeze. Omnipresent Mount Rainier stood tremendous and triumphant on the horizon beyond the school's brick buildings.

Maybe I'd been wrong earlier. Maybe western Washington weather sometimes did have a way of matching your mood.

Spencer shut off the car, and we both sat in contemplative silence as groups of kids walked by, chatting as they headed under the walkways and into the brick buildings. More students were back that day, and it seemed a little more laughter and playful screams rang across the school grounds than all of last week. No one would forget Emily Cooke and her untimely death. But maybe they were starting to move on, and things would get back to normal.

"Before I forget," Spencer said, "I wanted to say thank you."

I met his eyes. "Why?"

He smiled shyly and ducked his head. "Before yesterday, I thought I was going crazy. You proved I'm not, and you actually managed to learn a lot more about all this than I ever did. Also, you . . . you stayed with me last night when I was hurt, even with those shadow guys there."

"Oh." I bit my lip. "Well, you're welcome."

He chuckled, then climbed over his seat, leaning halfway into the backseat to grab his backpack. As he settled back into the driver's seat, I said, "And thank you, too."

"I didn't really do much."

"No," I insisted, "you did. You got the killer off me last night, remember? And, well, before this morning I felt like everything was going out of control, but then . . . I don't know, you sort of calmed me down. Helped make things feel not so totally nuts."

He didn't seem to know what to say to that. My arm began to tremble as I realized I might have just been a little too forthcoming.

"I mean," I stammered. "It's just that—"

Before I could speak further and make a fool of myself, I felt Spencer's arms around me, pulling me into a hug. I stiffened in surprise as he clenched me awkwardly over the stick shift. Then his scent—that natural pheromone of his that had invaded my brain and led me to him—swirled around my nose. I inhaled, and every part of me relaxed. I fell into the hug, wrapping my arms around his shoulders.

"We should talk more after school," he said, his voice muffled by my hair.

"Yeah, okay," I said. "Sure. Definitely. Though I should check with my dad. I'm pretty sure I'm still grounded for all my wacky party shenanigans."

Spencer let me go and smiled at me. Shaking his head, he opened his door and hopped out.

I didn't want to move from that seat. I wanted to sit there and relive that moment in my head forever and ever. I had just gotten a hug from a cute guy who seemed funny and smart. And oh yeah, who was also a werewolf, just like me.

Every part of me tingled, and I was pretty sure a whole colony of monarchs had set up shop in my lower intestine for all the fluttering happening there. Part of me wondered, was this just part of the BioZenith programming or whatever it was they had done to us? Had they designed their werewolves to find a preordained mate? If it wasn't for his smell, would I even like Spencer?

But right then, I really didn't care. I'd worry about the details of what Spencer being my "mate" would mean later.

It may have actually happened differently, but as I remember it, a cloud descended from that perfect blue sky, opened the car door, slipped underneath me, and floated me out of the car. I bobbed along on my cloud, out of the parking lot and halfway to school—until I saw Megan standing on the walkway leading to the main entrance, watching me with an unreadable expression.

At that moment, the cloud went to vapor and I fell solidly back to earth. I clutched my book bag close to my chest. Spencer was already at the entrance to the school, high-fiving Mikey Harris as though nothing out of the ordinary had happened to him. He threw his arms into the air, telling some sort of joke. The guys around him all busted a gut in response.

Megan glowered at Spencer and then me, and I knew that she'd seen us together.

I raised my chin and wound through the milling teens to stand next to her. "Hey," I said, my voice carried off by the hum of noise from the people around us.

"Hey," she said. "I came to pick you up this morning, but your dad said you'd already left."

And then, she actually smiled at me.

Taken aback, I didn't quite know what to say. I scanned Megan head to toe. Same blond hair that hung all the way down her back, same black jeans and shirt, same giant nose. The girl standing in front of me certainly *looked* like Megan. But this was not a reaction to my car-stealing and milkshake-drugging antics that I expected the real Megan to ever have.

She linked her arm through mine and started strolling up the walkway to the school entrance. Only then did her smile falter, and I realized that whatever goodwill facade she'd been forcing was not long for this world.

"I was expecting you to call me this weekend," she said, her voice rising higher. "After you made me go all the way to Seattle to get my car."

I stopped and pulled away. A couple of guys ran into me, muttering, "Watch it," as they walked past us into the school.

"Listen, Megan—," I said.

She interrupted me, crossing her arms. "You know, I expected you to make a bigger effort to apologize than just give me some money and expect everything to be better."

"Megan . . ."

"I spent the whole weekend waiting around for you, Emily," she spat. Her chest heaved as she got herself worked up, ready to unleash all the anger she'd held in all weekend. "While you went off and did whatever you're doing with your new friends."

"Megan!" I shouted. "Will you shut up for a second and listen?"

Stunned, she did just that, finally looking me in the eye. Nearby some other kids watched us, laughing at us behind their palms. I didn't care.

"Look," I said, lowering my voice and leading her off the walkway. "I know things have been weird lately, and I wish I could explain, but I'm still figuring it out. But you need to know one thing: You are the last person I would ever leave or hurt on purpose. I don't have any new friends that I'm going to abandon you for."

"What about *him*?" Megan's expression darkened.

"'Him'?" I repeated. "You mean Spencer?"

I stood on my tiptoes to see over the other kids. Spencer was no longer by the front doors. He'd probably headed off to class.

"Yeah," she said. "Is he your boyfriend now? Is that what all this stuff is about?"

"What? No!" I sighed. "Megan, I don't want to fight

with you. I don't want you acting like I'm some demon for, I guess, trying to be more . . . grown-up."

She snorted, but couldn't hide a small smile. "'Grown-up,' huh? Which means I'm not."

"That's not what I mean," I said. Megan didn't respond.

We stood together in a long, awkward silence. Ahead of me, there was a thud of leather against skin, and a girl cried out. I saw class president Tracie Townsend race out of the crowd and into the grass next to the walkway, brandishing a football that I guess had hit her in the face. She chased after a gawky guy wearing a too-big Seahawks jersey.

Finally I sighed once more. "Look, Megan, I *am* sorry. I promise you I am. Nothing that happened this past week is anything I ever expected to happen. And that includes taking your car. You're right, I should have called to apologize. I just . . ."

I trailed off. I didn't quite know how to finish, or to truly explain. Spencer and I, along with a few other kids I had yet to find, we shared a secret. A secret I didn't know if I could tell Megan.

But Megan had been my best and only friend for years and years. And, forgetting all the insanity of the weekend, I had missed her. I couldn't imagine not having her to talk to.

I swallowed. "Please, Megan, just . . . just accept my apology, will you? I can't imagine us not being friends."

She didn't respond, or even look me in the eye, for what felt like an eternity.

"Something is going on with you," she said softly. "Are you ever going to tell me what? Are you actually sick?"

"I . . . yeah," I said. "I am. But I think I figured it out. I think from now on, I'll be better."

Megan looked up at me, and I could see the disbelief in her eyes, but also hope. Because I knew Megan, and I knew her well: I was her only real friend, just as she was mine. And she didn't want to lose me, either.

"All right," she said. "Okay, fine. I accept your apology. But at some point, you're going to sit down and tell me everything that's been going on."

"Deal."

Side by side, we re-entered the stream of kids heading up the walkway to the school.

"One thing," she said as we walked. "If you ever— *ever*—do anything else to me like you did Friday night, I *will* cut you. Got it?"

I laughed. "Got it."

We reached the front doors just as the first bell rang. All the students who had mingled outside until the last minute rushed to their first classes. Megan and I were about to do the same, but something caught my eye.

"Actually, I'll head to class in a minute," I said to Megan.

"Just need a sec out here, okay?"

She regarded me curiously, then shrugged. "All right. See you in a few."

I left Megan and the crowd behind, strolling just off the walkway to the wall where the makeshift memorial to Emily Cooke and Dalton had sprouted up the week before. The ribbons on the pole nearby had started to come untied, the flowers were wilted, teddy bears were soaked with rainwater. Only the pictures seemed to have weathered the weekend unscathed, protected as they were behind laminate.

I pressed my fingers against the photo of Emily Cooke. I looked into her smiling blue eyes and whispered, "I did it. I got him."

I had wanted to flip the switch that would make me become a normal teenager. But this? This could prove to be so much better. And now I had someone who understood me. Someone who was like me, with whom I could share all these changes. Several someones, in fact.

Not everything was right in my life, not by a long shot. I still had so many questions about what was going on with me, and despite what I'd told Megan, I still didn't know if I would ever be able to control the wild behavior of my other selves. I still had a whole family who thought I was becoming someone else, and a best friend who didn't seem entirely convinced I was still the same person, and a whole school full of teenagers—specifically some incredibly popular cheerleaders—who thought I was the corporeal embodiment of Satan. Not to mention I had a nervous feeling that Jared's brief interrogation of me and Spencer that morning wouldn't be the last we heard from the police.

Yeah, life was changing for me all right. It was scary and exciting, painfully sad and blissful all at the same time. Nighttime Emily had proven reckless, brazen, sometimes out of control. The wolf me was something totally different altogether.

But Daytime, Nighttime, Wolftime . . . they were all me. Frightened and fearless and frightening, all in one body. I didn't have all the answers, wasn't quite sure where life was going to take me, if I would ever feel completely in sync with my selves. But standing in front of that photo of the other Emily, it didn't matter. I let the worry wash away.

The final bell rang then, shaking me from my thoughts. I turned to find the front walkway to the school completely empty, save for a few loose pieces of notebook paper fluttering across the lawn.

Gripping my backpack tight, I raced through the front doors to the school, sneakers squeaking over the linoleum. I started to race toward class—when two officious-looking people stepped out into the main hall, deep in discussion.

The woman, who I recognized as one of the office ladies, turned toward me, her eyes registering recognition. I expected a stern glare at my lateness, but instead she put a hand on the shoulder of the man next to her and gestured in my direction.

"That's her," I heard the woman say.

I stood rooted to the spot, not sure what was going on. My heart pounded—was this guy from the police? Had they figured it out? Did they know what I was?

The man turned to face me. He was mousy and thin, no taller than me. He wore an unexceptional gray suit that seemed a size too large for him. His brown hair was thinning, his wire-rimmed glasses tilted slightly off center.

The man left the office lady's side and came toward me, smiling.

"Emily Webb?" he asked me, his voice surprisingly deep despite his diminutive size.

I nodded, confirming. "Am I in trouble?" I asked. "I didn't mean to come in late, I was just—"

The man let out a gentle laugh and rested a hand on my shoulder. I squirmed uncomfortably.

"No, not at all," he said. "I was sent from the school district to talk converse, erm, *counsel* students like yourself who have been directly affected by all that's been going on lately."

Stepping back, out of his grasp, I said, "I haven't really been affected. I don't know why—"

The man shook his head. "We got a call from the police department about how you and another student discovered a man's, ah, *body* last night. A man who could have been the person responsible for Emily Cooke's untimely death. Of course we understand how that might be traumatizing."

Yeah. Just a little.

I didn't want to stand there anymore. I felt so exposed in the wide, empty green hall. It was just the two of us standing there now, me and the small man—the office lady had disappeared. It was eerily quiet, save for the distant sound of muffled voices leaking through closed classroom doors.

"Yeah," I said. "Yeah, that was . . . Look, I should probably get to class, Mr. . . . ?"

"Savage," the man said, not letting his kind smile drop. "You can call me Mr. Savage. And of course, your studies should come first. But you should come find me in the office after the school day is done."

"Sure," I muttered as I brushed past him and speed-walked down the hall toward my half-over homeroom. "See you around."

"I'm sure you will," Mr. Savage called after me. "There is much we should discuss."

The Vesper Company
"Envisioning the brightest stars, to lead our way."
- Internal Document, Do Not Reproduce -

Partial Transcript of the Interrogation of
Branch B's Vesper 1
Part 6—Recorded Oct. 31, 2010

Vesper 1 (V1): Looks like we've come full circle,
Mr. Savage. Because that week ended the day I met
you. Or at least who you pretended to be.

F. Savage (FS): [clears throat] I apologize for all
the initial deception, Emily, but like I've said—

V1: You did all this for my own good, yes, I've
been hearing that ever since you people put a gun
to my face and marched me into a truck.

FS: It's the truth, Emily, I swear to you it's the
truth.

V1: Are you sweating, Mr. Savage? I think you are.
I can smell you. You're afraid, and the stench is
totally nauseating.

FS: I—

V1: What did that text message say, Mr. Savage?

FS: Everything's under control, I—I—I—it's—

V1: What were those noises in the hall? Are things

not going as you planned? Did it turn out that you and your freak bosses and their shadowmen underestimated us . . . deviants?

[Chains clang and then make the sound of snapping as they are pulled apart. Screeching sounds as furniture is tossed aside.]

FS: Emily, please, please, I—

V1: You know, Mr. Savage, me and my friends thought about it, and we guessed that you weren't actually going to let us go. Because we know what you and the Vesper Company have been up to all this time. We know all about BioZenith and how we were made into vespers and what we were made for. I know that all the horrible, awful things that have happened have been because of you and the other deluded people like you. And so we're not going to sit here and take it. Not after you made me—you made me—

[There is a shuffle of loafers on linoleum.]

V1: You can't really run anywhere, Mr. Savage.

[A cacophonous boom. (NOTE: Go back and detail time stamp here to clarify that this is the moment the door to the interrogation room was blown off hinges. Will need to reconcile with video footage at later date.)]

Unidentified Female (UF): Going somewhere?

FS: I—I—I—I—please, I—

V1: Took you long enough, Amy.

UF: Well, we had some things to take care of.

FS: Please, please, I don't want to die, I was just doing my job!

V1: We're not going to kill you.

UF: We're not?

V1: No. Like I told him, I'm not a big fan of blood.

FS: Thank you, oh God thank you, I—

V1: You better hurry and get out of here before I change my mind.

[Running footsteps; FS leaving room.]

UF: Why did you let him go?

V1: Because I want him to go back to the people behind all of this. I want them to know what we're capable of.

UF: You know, Em, I underestimated you. You're not just an undercover skank, after all.

V1: Thanks, Amy.

UF: I mean it.

V1: So do I.

[Shuffling as the two move about the room.]

V1: Wait. Don't destroy any of that.

UF: But they have your conversation recorded, and all that you wrote, too.

V1: I know. And I want it that way. I want them to read every single page and see who I was. Then I want them to hear everything that happened today and know what they made me become. And I want them to be afraid.

UF: You're crazy, girl.

V1: Only a little bit. Hey, did you know that they call people like us deviants?

UF: Who? You wolves?

V1: No, you psychs too, maybe others. Any of their vespers that they didn't totally control. Guess that tells you what they think of their creations.

UF: [laughs.] Deviants. I sort of like it.

V1: Me too. Now shut that thing off and let's go. We've got others to break out, and the night only lasts so long.
[Rustling as the tape recorder is picked up. A click as the recorder is shut off.]

End of Partial Transcript of the Interrogation of Branch B's Vesper 1

ACKNOWLEDGMENTS

Getting the first part of Emily Webb's journey from my brain and into your hands was a long and sometimes tumultuous journey that couldn't have been completed without the help of many other very talented people. A special thank-you to Stacy Whitman, Nina Hess, Shelly Mazzanoble, and the rest of the Mirrorstone crew for helping me get the idea off the ground and for their continued support; to Michael Stearns for his endlessly excellent guidance, editorial or otherwise, and for tirelessly working with his fellow Upstart Crows to find this story a home; and to Kristin Daly Rens, Sara Sargent, and everyone else at Balzer + Bray for seeing me through to the finish line and for working hard to make this the best book it can be. Thank you all!